**Unable to w…
Mia launche…
and arrived …
as the prop…
slowly wound down and stopped.**

The door on the opposite side of the plane opened. Mia caught sight of a pair of long, sun-kissed, muscular legs, which jumped down and landed on large feet. Intrigued, she watched as the legs strode around the plane, eating up the distance with commanding ease. Then the owner came into full view, and an uncontrollable shock of electric delight raced through her, completely disarming her.

Mia's mouth dried. The intensity of his look made her feel stripped bare, and to her horror she dropped her gaze.

'I wasn't expecting a welcoming party. I'm Flynn Harrington. Pilot and doctor.' He grinned with the cheekiness of someone who had inside information. 'You must be Mia.'

'You're the island doctor?' She couldn't hide the shock and disbelief from her voice.

He didn't look like any doctor she'd ever met— and she'd met more than her fair share, personally *and* profession…

And no doctor …

Dear Reader

In June 2007 my family left our home on the south coast of Australia and we set off on a six-hour flight to the far north of the country. It was 6C in Melbourne and 33C in Darwin—hard to believe we were still in the same country, but it wasn't just the weather that was different. As we toured around the World Heritage Area of Kakadu National Park and swam in the waterholes of Litchfield Park we absorbed the vivid reds, yellows and browns of the outback. We learned all sorts of things about the land, the plants and animals, and what they all mean to the Aboriginal people.

A very special part of our holiday was a two-day trip to an island in the Timor Sea. Here we went hunting for turtle eggs, watched dugong at play and crocodiles surfing in the ocean! As I sat around the campfire I started to get an idea for a story. We had met a lot of people on our holiday and many had come from the south. I found myself asking, "Why would someone from the south be drawn to the isolation of this island?"

And that is how Mia and Flynn's story evolved. Set against the background of the Aborigines' love for their land and their own unique health issues, Mia and Flynn are on the island running from their individual demons. Both are determined to live a solo life but they discover that no matter where you are or how far you go, you can't outrun your past until you face it.

I hope you enjoy their story as much as I enjoyed writing it and that one day you too can take a trip to the far north of central Australia. It's an amazing place!

Love

Fiona x

THE DOCTOR CLAIMS HIS BRIDE

BY
FIONA LOWE

MILLS & BOON®
Pure reading pleasure™

All the characters in this book have no existence outside the imagination of the author, and have no relation whatsoever to anyone bearing the same name or names. They are not even distantly inspired by any individual known or unknown to the author, and all the incidents are pure invention.

First published in Great Britain 2009
Harlequin Mills & Boon Limited,
Eton House, 18-24 Paradise Road, Richmond, Surrey TW9 1SR

© Fiona Lowe 2009

ISBN: 978 0 263 86833 3

Set in Times Roman 10½ on 13 pt
03-0309-46097

Printed and bound in Spain
by Litografia Rosés, S.A., Barcelona

Always an avid reader, **Fiona Lowe** decided to combine her love of romance with her interest in all things medical, so writing Medical™ Romance was an obvious choice! She lives in a seaside town in southern Australia, where she juggles writing, reading, working and raising two gorgeous sons, with the support of her own real-life hero! You can visit Fiona's website at www.fionalowe.com

Recent titles by the same author:

THE PLAYBOY DOCTOR'S MARRIAGE PROPOSAL
A WEDDING IN WARRAGURRA
A WOMAN TO BELONG TO
THE FRENCH DOCTOR'S MIDWIFE BRIDE

To Gaye, with heartfelt thanks for the friendship, the walks along the river and the conversations that roam from laundry liquid to solving the world's problems!

Special thanks to Nellie, for generously sharing her experiences as a Remote Area Nurse.

CHAPTER ONE

'YOU still on city time, Sis.' Susie, one of the Kirri health workers, grinned widely, her teeth white against her chocolate-brown face.

Mia Latham sighed and twirled her hair up, welcoming the light breeze against her very hot and sweaty neck. Jamming her straw hat down hard, she scanned the outback-blue skies for the elusive light plane.

Nothing.

Not a faint dot in the distance, not even a bird. Just heat haze shimmering upwards against wisps of grey smoke from the dry-season fires. She forced her shoulders to relax while muttering, 'He said eleven o'clock and now it's almost one.'

'He on island time.' Susie leaned back contentedly against the shady eucalypt.

Mia turned and gazed at the sensible indigenous health worker. 'But I have an immunisation clinic all organised, and we're keeping people waiting.'

Susie gave her a bemused look. 'You got no clinic till plane brings vaccines.' She shrugged. 'So sit. You can't do nothing until the plane comes.'

Every cell in Mia's body rebelled at the practical words. Her 'to do' list magnified in her head, the print bold and black, bearing down on her, urging her to do *something*, anything, to make a dent in it. She'd wanted to be as up to date as possible for when she met the visiting doctor. But at this rate she'd be way behind and she hated having no control over the situation.

She stifled a huge scream of frustration and plonked down awkwardly in the shade next to Susie, her cargo shorts instantly filling with fine, brown dirt. *Just great.* She might still be on Australian soil but nothing about life up in the far far north of the country, nothing about life on this tiny island resembled anything she'd ever known.

She'd wanted a change. She'd badly *needed* change but today, her fifth day on the job as a remote area nurse on Kirra Island, left her wondering if what she'd come to was harder than what she'd left.

Impossible.

She wanted remoteness, wanted to work on her own and be as far away as possible from her old life. She just wanted to forget.

She fanned her face and took a long slug of water from the bottle that was a permanent part of her in this heat. And this was the dry season—winter. She didn't want to think about the dripping humidity just before the big wet.

'Hear that?' Susie inclined her head to the right.

Mia couldn't hear anything. It was so hot that even nature had gone quiet. 'No.'

'Listen with all of you,' Susie chided gently.

Mia let the heat roll over her, let the dust settle on her and strained to hear past the silence of the soporific midday malady. A faint buzzing vibrated in her ears. 'The plane?'

Susie nodded. 'That's right. Him coming now.'

Mia moved forward, preparing to stand.

Susie's workworn brown hand rested against her forearm, detaining her. 'Still five minutes, no hurry.'

She forced herself to sit back but most of her wanted to rush out onto the runway and start unpacking boxes the moment the plane had come to a complete halt. She'd never been very good at sitting back and waiting. Even when she'd known in her heart there was nothing she could do to help her mother, she'd hated the waiting. Waiting and watching her die.

The Cessna lined up with the runway and slowly descended, coming in over the thick mangroves and the eucalypts, its small black wheels bouncing on the asphalt, sticky with heat. The pilot immediately opened the window and gave a wave.

Unable to wait a moment longer, Mia launched herself to her feet, leaving Susie under the tree, and she arrived at the low cyclone fence just as the propellers of the plane slowly wound down and stopped. The door on the opposite side of the plane opened. Mia caught sight of a pair of long, tanned, muscular legs, which jumped down and landed on large feet. Feet clad in sturdy work boots with khaki socks that casually gathered down around solid ankles.

It wasn't the usual uniform of a pilot—they wore long navy trousers. No, these legs looked like they belonged to a bounty hunter, buffalo or crocodile hunter—a man who spent a lot of time outdoors.

Intrigued, she watched as the legs strode around the plane, eating up the distance with commanding ease. Then the owner came into full view and an uncontrollable shock of electric delight raced through her, completely disarming her.

At well over six feet, her crocodile hunter had the natural grace of a man at one with his surroundings, and it radiated from the top of his jet-black hair to the tips of his olive-skinned fingers, which gripped a large cooler in one hand and held a backpack in the other. Three-day stubble hovered around his smiling mouth, fanning out along a firm jaw. Dark brows framed intelligent hazel eyes, whose mesmerising gaze quickly took in his surroundings, acknowledged Susie with a wave and then centred in on her.

Mia's mouth dried. The intensity of his look made her feel stripped bare and to her horror she dropped her gaze. She took in his broad shoulders, which were covered by a shirt made from locally designed fabric. The emerald green and sea blue of the design accurately depicted the colours of the island's land and sea, and together they brought out a hint of green in his hazel eyes.

Desperately wanting to look further to what she suspected would be a washboard-flat stomach, her professionalism hauled her gaze upwards and with a quick, steadying breath she stepped forward, hoping she looked more dignified than she felt.

'I wasn't expecting a welcoming party.'

A rich, deep voice with the smoothness of velvet cloaked her, making her heart hiccough. She looked up into teasing eyes, the flecks of green and brown almost moving like crystals in a kaleidoscope.

Confusion overrode her body's unwanted tingling reaction to him, making her dizzy with bewilderment. 'Aren't you the pilot bringing in the vaccines? I got a message…'

'I'm Flynn Harrington. Pilot, deliverer of vaccines and doctor.' He grinned with the cheekiness of someone who had inside information. 'You must be Mia.'

Doctor? She wasn't expecting to meet the island's visiting doctor for another three days. Her calendar, left to her by her predecessor, had 'Doctor clinic' inked in red for Monday.

'You're the island doctor?' She couldn't hide the shock and disbelief from her voice. He didn't look like any doctor she'd ever met and she'd met more than her fair share personally and professionally. *And no doctor has ever made you tingle like that.*

'Yep, I'm the doctor for Kirra, Mugur and Barra.' He extended his long arm out behind him, lazily indicating the approximate direction of the other islands. 'I divide my time between all three.'

A swoosh of righteous indignation surged through her, quickly dousing the unsettling sensations that had shimmered along her veins. She'd just lost half her morning hanging around for him. 'But you're three days early and you're also two hours late!' The heat and waiting caught up with her. 'And what do you mean you don't usually have a welcoming committee? I was here two hours ago, as your message instructed, to collect the vaccines. The least you could have done was to send a message to say you were going to be late.'

His casual stance stiffened for a moment and then his shoulders relaxed. 'I'm sorry. I forgot that you'd still be city-wired. Usually the truck comes and picks me up the moment they hear the plane coming over. That way no one's left waiting around.' He started walking toward the truck.

The city-wired tag pricked her like barbed-wire and she folded her arms against the sensation in her chest as she jogged to keep up with his long-legged stride. 'Well, it would have been nice if someone had told me.' She threw her hands out in front of her. 'You for instance, or Susie. Why didn't Susie tell me the routine?'

He tilted his head, his brows slightly raised. 'Did you ask her?'

His quiet and reasonable tone sent a ripple of contrition through her, dampening her indignation. 'Ah, no. I think I said something like, "We have to be at the airport at eleven."'

He pulled a battered bushman's hat out of his backpack before tossing the pack into the tray of the truck. Then he carefully wedged the cooler under a hessian sack. 'That's why she didn't say anything. Kirri people don't say no to a request. Susie was happy to help you so she came. If a local doesn't want to do as you ask, well, they just avoid the issue by failing to turn up.'

He glanced down at her, his expression a mixture of understanding and humour. 'Beware the "I'll come back and do it" sentence—that actually means no.'

Mia wiped the back of her hand against her perspiration-soaked forehead and sighed. 'I've got so much to learn.'

Flynn smiled and dimples carved through the black stubble, giving him a renegade look. Perhaps her initial impression of a crocodile hunter hadn't been far off. Somehow she couldn't imagine him in a white coat, stuck inside the antiseptic corridors of a hospital down south.

'If you want to learn then we're happy to teach you.' His voice rumbled around her like distant thunder.

A slight tremble of unease rippled through her before her indignation surged back. 'What do you mean, *if* I want to learn? Of course I want to learn.'

He shrugged. 'Not everyone does. We get a lot of people up here. They arrive city-wired, city-savvy, ready to save the world as long as it can be saved their way.' He grinned at Susie, who'd wandered over from the shade of the tree now that it looked like they were ready to return to the clinic. 'And then they leave us, don't they, Susie?'

Susie nodded. 'Yep. Mia third nurse this year.'

Mia's chest tightened. 'I plan to be the one that stays.'

'Yeah, they all say that.' Flynn opened the driver's door of the truck, his expression resigned.

'No, really, I'm staying.' *I have nothing to go back to. Nothing at all.* Her mother's blank and expressionless face wafted across her mind and a sliver of the terror she usually managed to keep concealed deep inside her coiled upward, threatening to choke her.

She needed to move, she needed to *do* something to keep the panic at bay. *The clinic.* Walking briskly, she ducked under Flynn's outstretched arm and sat down hard in the driver's seat.

A startled expression momentarily creased his forehead before he gently closed the door.

A dash of guilt bubbled up at her abrupt brush past him but it was quickly doused by fear and anger at his blasé attitude toward her. She gripped the steering-wheel hard and breathed in deeply. How dared this man make assumptions about her when he didn't even know her? She wasn't 'everyone'. She was so far removed from being 'everyone', so far removed from being the 'norm', that it didn't bear thinking about.

She turned the key in the ignition and gunned the engine, clawing back some control. It was time get back to work.

She turned her head and met his clear and intense gaze. A shiver shot through her, making her both cold and hot at the same time. A shiver that created shimmers deep inside her. *No, no, no. Remember Steven.*

Don't remember Steven. She'd been working really hard on forgetting Steven and she didn't want to revisit that pain either.

She involuntarily swallowed before clearing her throat. 'I need to run this immunisation clinic so if you're ready, we'll leave now.'

Flynn wordlessly pushed back from the door where his arms had been resting. 'Let's head back, Susie.' He walked slowly around the twin-cab truck, opening the back door for the health worker, and clambered in next to Mia, tilting his hat forward as if he was going to take a nap.

Everything about him, every action and word powerfully stated that this man was in command of his world—completely and utterly. It was in stark contrast to Mia, who had the feeling she was only just hanging on by her fingernails. Coming to Kirra was supposed to give her some control, and at the very least control over her job. She didn't think that was too much to ask, given what she faced in the future.

Mia thrust the truck into gear, forcing away the thoughts that threatened to undo her. She refused to let 'Dr Cool and Laid-Back' make her feel incompetent.

You're doing a good enough job of that yourself.

With a jerk, she swung the truck into a wide U-turn and pulled onto the main road, a plume of dust rising behind her. One hundred metres later she slowed and peered out the windscreen, checking for incoming planes as the runway crossed the road.

'You're right, no planes.' The words sounded muffled from under the hat.

Exasperation whipped her. 'Really, and you can see clearly out from under that hat, can you?'

Susie giggled behind her.

He tilted the hat back and his eyes twinkled at her. 'Well, there are few holes in this old workhorse, but I can also hear. Combination of the senses, Mia.'

Susie's earlier words, 'Listen with all of you' played across her mind. She'd been happy to hear them from Susie. But not from Flynn. Everything about this doctor had her on edge.

Thank goodness she only had to put up with him until tomorrow and then he'd fly out of her life for another week.

As she turned the truck onto the coast road and headed toward the clinic, she had to slow the vehicle to a crawl. There were people in cars, trucks, on bikes and on foot, blocking the road in a mass of colour—their bright clothing vivid against their dark skin. 'I wonder what's happening?'

'Barge is in.' Susie spoke matter-of-factly as she hopped out of the truck.

'Friday's barge day.' Flynn wound down his window and high-fived some of the kids walking along the road.

Mia could see a big blue ship almost sitting on the shoreline, a large gangplank coming from the centre of its twin hull and resting on the red beach. She stared straight ahead at the party atmosphere in front of her as an ute, loaded with boxes, drove off the barge.

'And that means…' Flynn's mouth twitched at the corners but his eyes expressed commiseration.

Realisation thudded through her. 'It means no one is going to bring their baby, toddler or pre-schooler to the clinic this afternoon to be immunised.' She gently banged her forehead against the steering-wheel, defeat tugging at her every pore.

'See, you're catching on already.' His words were gentle with no trace of jubilation at her frustration.

With her head still against the wheel, she turned slightly as he stretched his long arms above his head, his shirt straining against muscular biceps. She bit her lip against the surge of unwanted heat that coiled through her. 'You didn't mention barge day when we left the airport.' Her voice wavered.

He shrugged, his face impassive. 'You were pretty

strung out at that point. I thought it best to go with *your* flow.'

She breathed in hard, realising she'd made a fool of herself in front of her new colleague. What did they say about first impressions not being able to be undone? She welcomed the uncomfortable edge of the steering-wheel against her forehead, overriding the pain of humiliation. 'What a waste of a day.'

'Nothing is ever a waste, Mia.' His soft words washed over her, not soothing but not gloating either. 'I tell you what, I'll fill you in as much as I can during the next week. At least you'll know that the footy and barge afternoons are times you do paperwork because no one will be at clinic.'

She abruptly sat up and stared at him, her heart hammering so hard against her ribs she was sure he could see it. Surely she'd misunderstood. Surely her humiliation wasn't going to be extended over one hundred and sixty eight hours. 'The next week?' Her voice squeaked out the words. 'I thought you were only here for tomorrow's clinic?'

He tilted his head to the side, his eyes crinkling in a smile. 'That had been the plan but things change. Kirra has the largest population so I'm here more often than not. I've been away for five days so now I need to play catch-up and I'm here for seven days straight.'

Somehow she managed to force the muscles of her face into a smile, while her gut seemed to fold inward. 'I guess it's my lucky week, then.' But luck had never played a role in her life and she didn't believe it was going to start any time soon.

CHAPTER TWO

FLYNN gazed out of his office window, watching the cabbage palms waving in the breeze and desperately trying to ignore the lure of the sunshine and wide-open spaces. Most of him wanted to be outside, swimming in a waterhole or just sitting under the shade of the banyan trees with the local community. He learned a lot by just sitting and listening.

But he had a major health department report due, and a budget review—two huge tasks that should be claiming his complete attention. Hadn't he told Mia that Friday afternoon was a good time for admin work? But it seemed he couldn't take his own advice today and his mind kept wandering. For some inexplicable reason he couldn't stop thinking about Mia.

A dull thud sounded behind him, the third bump in the last twenty minutes. It sounded like Mia was tearing apart the treatment room. He grinned despite himself. She was the type of woman who couldn't sit still even if she was tied to a chair. There was nothing new in that. Each new nurse needed to put his or her stamp on the place.

He met a new nurse every few months. More male

nurses were taking up positions but they were usually younger, came for some adventure, and headed back south for a promotion.

Generally the nurses were older women, jaded with life, anti-men, and they came up here so they could work solo. Teamwork didn't usually feature on their agenda and they 'tolerated' doctors in their domain. He was used to flying in, running his clinics and flying out. In between he consulted over the phone for emergencies and other than those contact times he rarely gave these competent women another thought.

But Mia, with her long blonde hair, her vivid blue eyes and high cheekbones, had caught his attention the moment he'd walked around the plane. She didn't fit the type at all. She seemed out of place and that had piqued his curiosity.

Yes, curiosity was the only reason he was thinking about her. It had nothing at all to do with honey-brown skin, a hesitant smile and long, long legs.

No, he was immune to women and had been since three thirty p.m., March eighteenth, two years ago.

But despite his immunity, the image of Mia—eyes flashing against fleeting shadows, with her hands fixed firmly on shapely hips—wafted across his mind. She'd been prickly from the moment they'd met.

The least you could have done was send a message to say you were going to be late.

She was bossy with a take-charge attitude. He laughed out loud, the sudden realisation pushing away the disconcerting feeling that had dogged him since he'd first seen her. Mia wasn't any different from the usual RAN after all.

With a clear mind he returned his attention to the spreadsheet blinking at him from the computer and tackled the budget.

Running feet unexpectedly pounded on the ramp outside his office and the door of the men's entrance to the clinic was abruptly flung open, its hinges screeching in protest.

'Doc, Sis, come quick.' The distressed voice bounced off the walls.

Flynn shot out of his chair, reaching the corridor at the same moment as Mia. He instantly recognised Walter, one of the talented wood carvers on the island. 'What's happened?

'What's wrong?'

Walter gripped the railing on the wall, panting hard. 'Jimmy, he's in the ute. He's hurt pretty bad.'

'I'll get the trolley.' Mia quickly disappeared into the treatment room.

Flynn picked up the emergency kit. 'Let's go.' He pushed open the door and ran, the heat of the late afternoon hitting him hard after the cool air of the clinic.

A twelve-year-old boy lay very still on his side in the back of a truck, the whites of his eyes wide with fear and a spear protruding from his back.

Flynn flinched at the unusual sight, immediately calculating possible internal damage. 'Thank goodness you left the spear in place, Walter.'

The man ran his hands through his tight, curly hair. 'Them boys were practising. I went to burn off, I was gone a few minutes and…' A long breath shuddered out of him as words failed him.

Flynn squeezed the father's shoulder. The rattle of the trolley wheels against the ramp sounded behind him, along with Mia's gasp as she stopped next to him.

This emergency would give him a chance to see Mia in action, and firm up what he already knew. Mia was cut from the same cloth as every RAN—a sole practitioner who had trouble working as part of a team. He'd worked with most types and sometimes it was easy and sometimes it was a hard slog. Based on how she'd bumped him from driving the truck, it would probably be a hard slog.

She cleared her throat. 'Right, we need to cut the spear down closer to the entry point before we move him. We don't want to cause any more damage than has already been done.' She spoke firmly, as her sound practice broke through her initial shock. She looked straight at Flynn. 'We need a saw.'

Flynn swallowed a sigh. She'd immediately taken charge, directing the play despite the fact she was working with a doctor. Situation normal. It looked like the power struggle had started already. 'Walter, we need to cut the spear. Can you get a saw or some strong secateurs?'

'I'll get them from the shed.' The anxious father ran around the building to the bush medicine garden, which was an important part of tying in indigenous medicine with modern.

'There's packing gauze in the kit to steady around the puncture site.' Flynn handed Mia the large box, expecting her to counter his request with a suggestion of her own.

'Right, will do.' She eagerly accepted the box and pulled on a pair of gloves.

Her unexpected compliance startled him but there

was no time to second-guess her. He needed to concentrate on Jimmy. He crawled into the back of the ute, the ribbed metal hard against his knees. 'Hey, mate, you weren't supposed to be the target in practice. How are you feeling?' His fingers immediately rested on the young boy's neck, feeling for his carotid pulse.

Jimmy bit his lip, trying hard to be stoic. 'It hurts heaps.'

Flynn nodded in understanding as he silently counted Jimmy's pulse. Rapid but firm. Perhaps the spear had missed vital organs? But most of him knew that was probably wishful thinking.

Metal pinged as Mia scrambled onto the tray, hauling the emergency kit with her. 'Hi, Jimmy, I'm Mia and I'm going to have to touch the area around the spear but I'll be as gentle as I can.'

She smiled at their patient and for the first time since Flynn had met her, her face lost its tension and her eyes shed their shadows.

It changed her completely. Unexpected heat charged through him and he had a momentary vision of her standing on a beach with her long hair trailing out behind her and her face lifted up to the breeze—with not a care in the world.

What the—? Where on earth had that thought come from? He shoved the image aside and reminded himself that she was the island nurse, pure and simple.

Mia deftly wrapped the gauze around the puncture site with gentle care. 'You're being very brave, Jimmy.'

Jimmy fixed his eyes on her face, hanging onto her murmured words like a lifeline.

Flynn didn't blame him. There was something about

her that could keep a bloke mesmerised, but not him. He reminded himself of his cast-iron immunity, the one that Brooke had activated.

'Flynn, I got a bush saw.' Walter ran up holding a bright orange-handled saw.

'Thanks, Walter, excellent work.' Flynn took the proffered saw.

Mia immediately opened a sterile pack and covered the gauze she'd placed around the spear entry point with a small theatre towel. 'We don't need wood shavings in there as well. I hope you're as good with a bush saw as you are with a scalpel.' She gripped the spear firmly at the entry point and glanced up at him, giving a quiet, companionable smile.

A completely unexpected smile.

He found himself smiling back. 'I've improved with practice.' He tapped the back of his hand where a long, jagged scar ran across three knuckles.

'Ouch.'

'My seven stitches were a badge of honour but Dad didn't let me loose in the carving shed after that. Right, holding tight.' The large bush saw seemed ludicrous against the narrow width of the spear but it was all they had. And he was used to making do. Medicine in remote rural communities was as much about improvisation as it was about modern medicine. He placed the bush saw a couple of centimetres above her hand.

Her hand tightened on the spear. 'You need to leave more room.'

He tamped down his frustration at her tone. 'I know what I'm doing, your knuckles will be safe.'

'I'll hold you to that.' She spoke softly and flicked her gaze to his, sea-blue irises sparkling at him like sunshine on water.

His heart rate unexpectedly kicked up for the first time in a very long time, pushing delicious languid heat through him, warming places that had been cold since Brooke's betrayal.

His hand instantly gripped the saw harder, willing the sensation away. He refused to accept the feeling, hating that it could even happen after two years of self-imposed celibacy. Forcing his attention to the spear and the saw, he spoke slowly. 'Jimmy, I'm going to cut the spear. I need you to keep as still as possible.'

He carefully pulled the serrated silver blade through the wood and five quick cuts later, the spear was in two pieces.

Mia checked Jimmy's pulse and stroked his head. 'You're doing really well.'

The boy whimpered.

Flynn touched the boy's shoulder. 'Jimmy, we're going to slide you onto a trolley and take you inside.'

'I'll steady his hips, you take his shoulders and, Walter, you can take the feet.' Mia raised herself from kneeling to a low squat, ready to move, and gave Flynn an expectant look. 'On your count, Flynn, when you're ready.'

She'd taken over again. 'Thanks for that.' He couldn't stop the sarcasm leaking into his voice.

Mia blinked against a flash of confusion and a slight frown creased her forehead.

You're being petty. He shut his ears to the voice and crawled around behind Jimmy's head, putting his arms under the boy's left shoulder. 'One, two, three.'

The young boy bit his lip as he was carefully slid down the tray on his side and then lifted onto the trolley.

'We need you to lie very still on your front.' Their voices collided, deep resonance tumbling with gentle softness.

Mia shrugged her shoulders, a wry smile hovering around her mouth. 'What can I say? I'm a firstborn and we always tend to take charge.'

His mouth twitched despite him wanting to keep a straight face, the truth of her comment hitting home. 'You and me both.'

A trickle of laughter sprinkled her words. 'Oh, dear, we could be in strife, then. All chiefs and no Indians.' Her smile expanded, dancing down into the deep creases that formed around her plump mouth.

Irrational disappointment streaked through him when she looked away and spoke to Jimmy.

'Are you OK?'

'Just OK.' Jimmy's scared voice was barely audible.

'Walter, go and get Ruby.' Flynn knew the father wouldn't want to be in the clinic and the boy needed his mother.

'I'll bring her.' The stressed man hopped into the truck and drove off.

'Let's go.' Flynn flicked the brakes on the trolley upward with his foot, releasing the wheels, and together he and Mia quickly pushed the trolley inside.

'How about I prime the Hartmann's and insert the IV while you examine him?' Mia ripped open an IV set and plunged the metal-tipped top into a bag of electrolyte fluid.

He caught the subtle change in her tone. She'd tried to convert her 'in-charge' statement into a question. 'Good idea.' He had to agree with her—the division of jobs was in Jimmy's best interests.

He pulled his stethoscope off the hook and pushed it into his ears. He listened intently to the air entry, even though the puncture wound was probably lower than the lungs. Who knew which direction the spear was lying internally?

'Jimmy, I need to put a needle into your arm so we can give you something to drink through your veins.' Mia wrapped the tourniquet around Jimmy's thin, left arm. 'I promise it will hurt a lot less than the spear.'

The boy squeezed his eyes shut as if he didn't want to think about it.

'Air entry good, respirations slightly elevated.' Flynn wrapped the blood-pressure cuff around the boy's arm and listened to the sound of the whoosh and thump of the blood pounding in the arteries. He swung the stethoscope around his neck. 'BP's dropping slowly. He's bleeding somewhere.'

'Or leaking somewhere?' Her brows drew together in concentration as she examined Jimmy's arm. 'He's not exactly in shutdown but some of his veins have collapsed.'

'A slow bleed.' He mulled over the idea, enjoying having someone to talk to about a diagnosis.

She tapped the sluggish vein on the boy's arm, her eyes glued to the spot. The tip of her pink tongue ran across her top teeth in an action of pure concentration.

Flynn's gaze zeroed in on her lush, red lips, the moist tongue holding his gaze like a magnet. An age-old surge of lust—hot, hard and intense—rocked through him so unexpectedly he almost staggered.

Her mouth closed and with practised care she slid the wide-bore cannula into the dark vein just below his elbow. 'I'm in—line established.'

Her words broke over him and it was like being released from a trance. What was wrong with him today? He didn't react like this. He knew only too well it led to heartache and loss. He cleared his throat and spoke gruffly. 'Great. Give him five hundred millilitres stat while we work out what's going on.'

He bent down so his face was close to his patient's. 'Jimmy, I have to roll you onto your side for a moment so we can put some dots on your chest.'

'Why?' The young lad gripped the trolley's mattress.

'So we can see your heartbeat on the screen.' Mia pointed to the ECG machine. 'It's pretty cool to watch.'

'Will you help me?' Jimmy asked Mia.

'Of course I will.' Mia smiled down at him.

'But it hurts to move.'

The plaintive wail tore at Flynn. 'I know, mate, and as soon as I've examined you I can give you something for the pain. You just have to be brave for a bit longer, OK?'

Jimmy's brown curls bobbed sadly as he nodded his acquiescence.

'You steady his hips and protect the spear while I fix the dots,' Flynn instructed.

Mia nodded and quickly placed her hands into position. 'Ready when you are.'

Flynn tore the backing paper off the dots in preparation. 'One, two, three.'

Mia eased Jimmy into position with a smooth movement and a worried frown. A frown which carved three horizontal lines across the bridge of her nose, giving her a pixie look that clashed with her competent 'in-charge' persona. Nothing about this woman matched up or made sense.

Nothing about your reaction to her makes sense either.

With speed borne of experience, it only took Flynn a minute to have Jimmy connected to the ECG. 'And roll him back.' He didn't look at Mia, he wasn't risking any more crazy lust-fuelled reactions. Instead, he stared at the ECG and the ever-increasing pulse rate.

'Well done, Jimmy.' Mia stroked his head. 'You're doing so well.'

'Where's my dad?'

'I'm here.' Walter rushed through the door, quickly followed by Jimmy's mother, Ruby.

'Good timing, Walter.' Flynn tilted his head toward Jimmy. 'Ruby, you get up near Jimmy's head and stay with him. He needs his mum.'

Ruby didn't speak, she just moved quietly beside her son, her hand gripping his.

Walter immediately backed out of the room to wait outside.

Flynn pulled the stethoscope from his ears, having just taken Jimmy's blood pressure again. 'His pressure's still dropping slowly.' He turned up the drip rate on the IV.

'Do you want plasma expander?' Mia quickly wrote the current IV bolus on the fluid balance chart.

The thought had crossed his mind a moment before

she'd spoken. She certainly knew her emergency medicine. 'I'll keep it as an option. I'll do the ultrasound and then reassess.'

'Pethidine first?' Mia half turned toward the drug box.

He raised his brows. 'Mind-reading again?'

She nodded slowly. 'It's what I do.'

Her deadpan expression made him want to laugh. He realised she had a knack of being right without being dogmatic. 'Ruby, any idea how much Jimmy weighs?'

The worried mother silently shook her head.

'We just done that at school for maths. I was forty-five kilograms.' Jimmy's voice sounded muffled against the trolley mattress.

'Good going, mate. Thanks.' He gave Jimmy a reassuring pat before turning back to Mia, who was priming the pump. 'Given we're not sure what is bleeding or not, it's best to be cautious. We don't need him going into respiratory distress as well.'

'So...zero point two five per kilogram rather than zero point five?' She flicked back some stray hair from her face and then slowly brought the back of her hand under her chin in a caress of concentration as she worked out the dose.

The action mesmerised him and he was horrified to find he was staring. 'Yes, I'll draw it up.' He seized the proffered needle and syringe and concentrated on opening the ampoule, drawing up the solution, cross-checking the dose with Mia and injecting it into a small bag of saline.

Concentrating on the job rather than speculating on the intriguing nurse working next to him who wasn't fitting at all into the power-hungry, bossy role he'd assigned her at the start of the emergency. 'Jimmy, you might start to feel a bit sleepy.'

The pulsometer pinged loudly and Mia rechecked Jimmy's blood pressure. 'It's steadied but still too low.' She turned on the oxygen and carefully placed the prongs in Jimmy's nostrils. 'You just breathe normally, Jimmy, OK?'

The lad silently accepted the elastic being put around his head and gripped his mother's hand more tightly.

'How's that spear hurt him?' Ruby spoke for the first time.

Flynn pulled the ultrasound machine into place and squirted gel onto Jimmy's back. 'That's what we're going to find out.'

The black and white swirl of the ultrasound slowly morphed from a snowstorm into clear vision. Flynn's eyes adjusted to the images on the screen.

'It always looks like fuzz to me.' Mia gave a self-deprecating chuckle from the other side of the trolley.

Her candour startled him. He wasn't used to people publicly admitting what they didn't know. He tilted the screen so she could see it and pointed to a white shape surrounded by black. 'Recognise that?'

She peered toward the screen. 'Is that the spear? I thought it would show up as black.'

'It's solid so it reflects a greater amount of sound or echo and it gives out a more intense signal which shows up as white.' A familiar surge of satisfaction welled inside him—he'd always enjoyed teaching staff when he'd been down south.

'That makes sense. Thanks for explaining it.' Smile lines curved around her mouth for a moment before fading.

She's open to learning.

He ignored the unwanted voice of reason. Holding up his fingers ten centimetres apart, he spoke to Ruby. 'It's gone inside Jimmy that much.'

Ruby silently absorbed the information, her eyes glued to the screen.

He slowly explored the peritoneum, heart, dia-phragm, the liver, spleen, kidneys and bowel, looking for signs of black and grey, which would indicate fresh bleeding. 'It's torn a small hole in the liver.'

'Would that account for his BP?'

Flynn rubbed his chin, enjoying having such an inter-ested colleague. 'Perhaps, but it's not a big hole and a haematoma's already forming.'

'I need to pee.' Jimmy started to wriggle.

Mia quickly grabbed a urinal and a privacy sheet, and helped the boy get into position to void.

'Test it, Mia.'

'I thought I might.' The words hung in the air as she walked out with the filled bottle.

Her soft and reasonable tone at his unnecessary order slugged him. Nurses always tested urine and he had no idea why he'd even said it, especially as they'd seemed to settle into a truce of sorts and were working together quite well.

Because she's got under your skin.

He turned his attention to the examination of Jimmy's right kidney. It was the organ closest to the liver and as the liver had been nicked, there might be damage there. The kidney came into focus.

'Flynn, he's got gross haematuria, his urine is pink. Can you see signs of bleeding on the ultrasound?' Mia's voice carried across the room.

He tilted his head. 'Come and look at this.' He pointed to the image of Jimmy's right kidney, which showed a small tear at the top. 'It's sliced through the top of the kidney, torn the liver and come to a halt.'

She leaned in close and he caught the scent of sun and sand, with a hint of the heady perfume of frangipani. He stifled the urge to breathe in more deeply.

'Will he need surgery to repair the tears?'

He kept his eyes on the screen, checking he hadn't missed anything. 'I think that the haematoma will stop the bleeding. To a certain extent it already has because his pressure's steadied and the kidney and liver should heal just fine on their own.'

'So we can remove the spear tip safely now without fear of causing a big bleed?'

He turned to face her. 'We can.'

'That's excellent news.' Happiness for their patient radiated from her and her face glowed. 'After a few days of close monitoring he'll be back kicking the footy.'

Flynn deliberately looked away from her smile, trying to stall the rush of blood to his groin. He caught sight of the protocol handbook resting on the desk. Written by bureaucrats in Darwin and issued to every new health-care worker, Mia must have been reading it before Jimmy's arrival. 'Technically, the clinic doesn't allow for overnight stays and any major medical emergency should be evacuated.'

Again Mia frowned, the bridge of her nose wrinkling. 'Surely he'd be better off here close to his family. I'm happy to nurse him and you're on the island if his condition unexpectedly deteriorates.' Her eyes suddenly teased. 'I'll toss you for the three a.m. to five shift.'

He smiled broadly. 'You're on.' He couldn't believe his luck—she knew her medicine *and* she was prepared to bend the rules. The Kirri people hated leaving the island and Ruby would be out of her depth in Darwin.

'For two firstborns, we seemed to manage that pretty well, didn't we?' She spoke quietly, suddenly serious.

The look in her deep aqua eyes whipped him hard in the gut. A look that was devoid of any grandstanding, the look that was completely inclusive and said loudly, *We're a team.*

A team. She was right—they had worked well together. He should be thrilled that after all this time he was finally working with a RAN who wanted to be a team player because that would make his working life so much easier. But a leaden feeling settled in his gut and thrilled didn't come close to describing it. He ran his hand through his hair, his brain scrambling to make sense of his feelings.

She's just an average nurse like every other one you've met, worked with and forgotten.

But there was nothing average about Mia and that was the problem.

CHAPTER THREE

FLYNN walked over to the clinic from his residence, smelling the salt lingering on the early Saturday morning air, and breathed in deeply, savouring the freshness. Not one breath of wind rippled the trees and he knew the sea would be flat and calm—an ideal morning to go fishing.

He had a patient to see and a patient to hopefully discharge and then the day was his, emergencies notwithstanding. He'd ask around and perhaps drive up to the north of the island and see if anyone was heading out to fish. He could do with a day away from the clinic.

A day away from Mia. He needed to clear his mind.

He shoved his hands deep into his pockets. He should have taken the three to five a.m. shift for all the sleep he'd got. Images of Mia had floated through his mind despite him trying to shut them out, despite practising deep breathing and attempting relaxation. Hell, he'd come to these islands to avoid women and life had been easy. He wasn't going to let one nurse change that.

As he pushed the clinic door open he heard Jimmy calling out.

'Mia, is there more toast?'

Relief settled over him. He'd made the right decision in not evacuating Jimmy. A boy with a healthy appetite was a great sign.

Mia appeared from the kitchen holding a tray with cereal, milk and fruit. 'Good morning.' A warm smile tinged with familiar tension washed across her face. 'I hope you ate breakfast at home because the way Jimmy is eating, my supplies are dwindling at a rapid rate.'

Her tinkling laugh spun around him, pulling at him with its intoxicating, sweet sound. For a woman who'd been up half the night she had no right to look so fresh and alluring. Her face, free from make-up, shone with a healthy glow, and her hair framed her cheeks, not yet pulled back into its usual neat ponytail.

He'd called into the clinic at three a.m. but Jimmy had been stable and sleeping and she'd sent him away, promising to catch a few hours' sleep herself. He took the tray from her. 'I learned the hard way and now I have a secret stash of food.'

'Ah, yet another trick of remote medicine I have to learn.' She pulled a tiny spiral notebook and pencil out of her pocket and wrote 'Food supplies' in it, under a list of other short notes, the bridge of her nose creasing in concentration.

The action surprised him. He'd understand if she wrote down a reminder for a drug order or something related to work, but some extra food?

She caught him staring at her and she quickly flicked the notebook closed, jamming it back in her pocket as if caught out doing something wrong. 'Let's give the boy round three of his breakfast.'

Jimmy sat crossed-legged on the bed, crumbs scattered all around him.

'Is that all that's left of three slices of toast and Vegemite?' Mia teased as she brushed away the crumbs. 'I had a brother who had hollow legs like you. He used to eat and eat and eat.'

Flynn slid the tray onto the over-bed table, wondering about the words 'had a brother'. Wouldn't people normally say, 'My brother used to have hollow legs like you'? 'Tuck into this, mate, and then I'll come back and have a look at your dressing, OK?'

Jimmy bit into a yellow banana and nodded as Flynn motioned for Mia to leave the room with him.

He strode into the kitchen and plugged in the coffee-machine. 'I need a cappuccino—what about you?'

'That sounds great.' Mia cut two slices of hearty wholemeal bread and dropped them into the toaster. 'So, will Jimmy be discharged home to rest today or do you want to keep him in a bit longer so that his wound can be kept clean and dry?'

Flynn glanced at her over the top of the opened fridge door, knowing what she was really asking. 'Have you done many home visits yet?'

She nodded, her teeth snagging her bottom lip. 'A few. I've worked in disadvantaged areas in Tasmania but I was pretty shocked by the state of some of the houses here and the overcrowding.'

He closed the fridge and at the same time tried to close his mind against the vulnerable image of pearly white teeth on pink, moist skin. The milk slopped into the jug rather than being poured. 'Yeah, the poverty is confronting. Over twenty per cent of the houses need replacing but the good news is that the land council is on target with their three-year plan to replace and build new ones.'

'That's great but I guess what I'm really asking is does Jimmy live in a condemned house? We can't risk him getting a raging infection and damaging his kidney.'

'True, but Jimmy's very fortunate. Both his parents have jobs and although there are ten people in the house, Ruby has it well organised.' He placed the jug under the stainless-steel steam jet and heated the milk. 'We'll get Ruby to bring him in each day and you can do the dressing. That way he can be at home but we can keep a close eye on him.'

The toast popped up and Mia put the slices on plates and buttered them. 'OK, so I'll remove his IV after breakfast. Do you want one last dose of IV antibiotics first?'

'Yes, that's a good way to do it and then he can go home with a seven-day course.' Flynn poured the foaming milk over the coffee, picked up the mugs and turned to see Mia writing again in her notebook. 'Discharge planning?'

She gave a curt nod, the shadows in her eyes suddenly looming large. She shoved the pad into her pocket as if the fact it was out of sight meant it no longer existed. 'Thanks for the coffee. Help yourself to toast.'

Her reaction to the notepad puzzled him but the delicious smell of the toast distracted him and he bit into it, enjoying the combination of seeds and grains. He hadn't tasted bread like this on any of the islands. 'This tastes sensational. Where did you order it from?'

She looked coy. 'I baked it?'

'You made this? No wonder Jimmy virtually inhaled it. He's probably never tasted bread like it. We only get the mass-produced loaves sent over from Darwin.'

She gave a wry smile. 'And that's why I brought my bread-maker.'

An idea struck him. 'This would be fabulous bread for the diabetics due to its low-glycaemic index. Is there any way you could work out how to cook it on a campfire?'

Disbelief swept across her face. 'A campfire? Why a campfire? I've seen ovens in houses.'

He shrugged. 'Many Kirri people prefer to cook on open fires.'

'I thought they'd only cook on a fire when they're out bush, hunting or collecting bush tucker.'

'They do that too but there's a campfire in every yard. It's an easier way to cook when you never know how many people are going to be eating with you.'

She sighed. 'There are so many unexpected things. For instance, I didn't realise that English would be the second or third language. It's all so very different, but different in a good way.'

He nodded as an unexpected sensation of shared companionship streaked through him. 'And that is what most southerners just don't get.'

She reached for her pocket but caught his gaze, which had followed her movement. She let her hand fall back onto the table and fiddled with the mug handle, anxiety scudding across her eyes. 'I'll practise and see how the bread comes out unleavened, kind of like a wholemeal damper.' He saw the thought travel across her high cheeks as her mouth curved into a smile. 'If it doesn't work, the kids could use it as a football.'

He laughed. 'Either way, they'd be happy. Football is the second religion on the island.' He knew she wanted to write 'Damper' down in that notebook of hers but had deliberately stopped herself. Why, he didn't know and he really shouldn't care. He should be thinking about getting out of here and going fishing.

A strained and unexpected silence expanded between them, vanquishing the companionable conversation that had existed when they'd been talking about work.

Mia pushed her chair back, her shoulders suddenly rigid with tension. 'I'll get the dressing trolley ready and give those antibiotics. See you when you've finished your coffee.' She walked out of the room, her three-quarter-length pants moving seductively across a pert behind.

A wave of heat hit him hard and hot, and he stood up abruptly, trying to stall it. It didn't work. All that happened was that he knocked over his chair. What the hell was going on with him?

He'd specifically chosen this remote region to avoid women and the nightmare of relationships. It had been working really well for two years. He'd carved out a life of work and sport and he was content with his lot. He didn't want or need anything else.

His life was just as he wanted it.

So his reaction to Mia made no sense at all. He'd mark it down as an aberration.

A tall and curvaceous aberration.

He nuked the traitorous thought with an undisputable fact. Conversation between them died once they'd exhausted talking about work. Given the strained silence that had built between them once they'd finished talking shop, they obviously had nothing in common.

At least he'd worked that out quickly. That would kill this insane attraction dead in its tracks. Today he was going fishing and by the time Monday came around he would have got over whatever it was that was making him feel like a randy seventeen-year-old and Mia would be just another RAN.

'Flynn?'

He turned from the sink. 'Hi, Walter. Good news. Jimmy can go home today but he has to rest. Is Ruby with you?'

'Yeah. She's with Mia.' Walter continued to stand in the doorway, his head down, avoiding eye contact in the traditional way.

Flynn had learned over time that just standing often meant the person wanted to say more. He turned back to the sink so he wasn't looking straight at Walter and he waited. The two hardest lessons he'd learned since arriving on Kirra had been waiting and listening.

'Mia did good with Jimmy.'

Flynn washed the coffee-mugs. 'She did. She knows her stuff.'

'Yeah.'

'Any of your mob going fishing today?' Flynn flicked the teatowel off the silver rail.

'No.' Walter moved his foot in circles against the lino. The brevity of answers was another thing he'd got used to. 'I thought I'd go. I fancy some barramundi for dinner.'

Walter shook his head. 'No fishing today, Flynn. We got a ceremony.'

Surprise rushed through him. Usually he knew about the ceremonies and often he was invited to be part of them. 'OK, well, I guess I'll have to chance the fishing on my own, then.'

'The ceremony is for Mia so you have to come, and bring her with you.' Walter turned and left, walking outside to wait for Ruby and Jimmy.

Flynn's chest tightened as the reality of Walter's request hit him. He had no choice—he had to go to the ceremony. He couldn't refuse Walter's request. As an elder on Kirra, Walter had made Flynn a 'brother', teaching him many of the Kirri ways. It was a relationship that was very special to him and one that helped with his work on the island.

Images of his quiet day fishing, his day of relaxation and regrouping, burst like a balloon.

Mia.

Instead of fishing, he would have to spend the day with Mia at the ceremony. Mia, who was wound so tight she threatened to implode at any moment. And without work to talk about, there'd be those long, anguished silences.

It was going to be a really long day.

Mia silently chanted some important details in her head while she walked alongside Flynn, his long strides sending tiny whirls of dust up into the air. The sun was rising high in the sky, promising even more heat later in the day, and already she could feel the familiar trickle of perspiration down her back.

She ached to write up her daily report and a note to herself about the bread, but Flynn had unexpectedly but firmly insisted she lock up the clinic and come with him straight away.

She supposed she could have asked him to wait five minutes but the inquisitive and bemused look he'd given her earlier that morning when she'd pulled out her notebook had made her hesitate. She didn't want to have to justify why she kept notes on almost everything. Unless someone had lived with a parent who had slowly and insidiously lost their memory, they just didn't understand.

Lists had become part of her life. Initially they had been there to help her mother. Now they were her life-lines, her attempt to stave off the inevitable.

Working with Flynn had been very different from what she'd expected. They'd managed a co-operative approach, which had been a pleasant surprise. And he'd taken the time to help her decipher the ultrasound. He was a natural teacher and she planned to drain his brain while he was on the island to her advantage. The faster she learned and the more she knew meant her position at Kirra was secure.

And thinking of Flynn in terms of a teacher was a *lot* less disturbing to her equilibrium than thinking of him as a man. She glanced up at him from under her straw hat. He radiated such boundless energy despite his apparently laid-back approach to life. Bright board shorts had replaced yesterday's pleated shorts, and today he wore a pink and black shirt with a local design reminiscent of the palm leaf. He looked like he belonged on a beach or riding a wave.

An image of salt water running in rivulets over a broad chest slammed into her, sucking the air from her lungs and causing her to stumble.

A large hand firmly closed around her elbow, sending ribbons of sensation spiralling through her.

His eyes flickered with amber lights as he looked down at her. 'You have to keep an eye out for rocks and potholes. The roads here aren't in the best condition.'

'Thanks.' She smiled, trying to act relaxed and calm despite the fact she'd never felt so unnerved around a man in her life. Her body seemed to go into a 'hyper-awareness zone' whenever they were together. It completely drained her of energy.

Yesterday, as they'd dealt with Jimmy's accident, she'd lurched between clear-cut professional admiration and straight-up, bone-melting desire. The combination made her head spin. 'So, are we doing a home visit?'

'No.' He dropped his hand from her arm and pointed to a gathering of people. 'We're going to a ceremony.'

'Cool.' She stopped walking as a thought struck her. 'Is it culturally sensitive for us to go?'

He smiled, dimples carving into his cheeks. 'It's very OK for us to go. You're the guest of honour.'

She stared at him, her mind emptying of everything as his smile shone above her, driving out the darkness that cloaked her soul. Then his words echoed in her head, forcing her to speak. 'Me?' She struggled to think past the black hole that was her stalled and uncoopera-tive brain. 'But why me?'

'For helping Jimmy.'

Amazement flooded her that the community would do something like this. She'd never had such an acknowledgment in her working life. 'But I only did my job.'

'And the locals want to say thank you.' He stood waiting for her to move, a patient smile on his face as if he dealt with stunned women every day of the week. 'Come on, I'll introduce you to people.'

Men and women were sitting around, some on upturned milk crates, some on chairs, and a few on the ground. At their feet yellow and red ochre and white chalk was being mixed with water on large, flat rocks. A couple of old mirrors were passing around the circle so they could see their faces to paint them.

'Hey, Mia, we dance for you.' Walter waved to her, his eyes ringed with red ochre, edged with chalk.

She waved back before turning to Flynn. 'What can you tell me about the face painting? The designs look pretty intricate.'

He tilted back his hat. 'It's really body painting. Today they'll decorate their faces and arms but in a full ceremony they'd paint all their bodies. It's been practised for thousands of years and the design is passed down from generation to generation, from father to son.'

She watched fascinated as the dancers prepared themselves. 'The dots on their faces and the fine crossed lines on their arms—I saw that design on their carving and on your shirt yesterday.'

Flynn nodded. 'That's right—it's called crosshatching. Their traditional body art and the decoration on their traditional carving form the basis of today's screen-printing and artwork. It's all connected with their creation story.' He spoke warmly, his enthusiasm for the topic obvious. 'Their dreaming dance is handed down from their fathers too and it can be naturally occurring things like a crocodile, shark or wind, but some have a sailing boat.'

She glanced at him in surprise. 'A sailing boat?'

He spread his hands out in front of him. 'Probably from the first time the Europeans sailed past.'

She loved learning about these sorts of things. 'What about mothers? Is anything passed on from the mothers?'

He grinned. 'Your feminist side will be thrilled to know that they inherit their skin group and totemic dance from their mothers. This is often an animal like the magpie goose or brolga, but it could be scaly mullet fish.'

'I've been amazed at the number of geese. Their honking keeps me company at night.' *As do thoughts of you.*

He chuckled. 'The locals love that sound as it means there is plenty of good hunting.'

She walked over to the shade and sat down on the ground. She was immediately struck by how quickly she was losing the expectation that to sit required a chair. 'I'm slowly getting a handle on the skin-group issue. Who can talk to whom and who can't talk to each other.' She grimaced, suddenly remembering her forgetfulness.

He tilted his head, taking in her expression. 'Problem?'

She traced her finger through the fine dirt. 'Oh, it's just that I had a lapse the other day when I made the mistake of asking a fourteen-year-old boy to give a message to his mother, forgetting he can't talk to her. I've now put up the skin group compass on my wall so I always remember.'

Understanding wove across his face. 'Don't be too hard on yourself. It seems complicated at first because it's so foreign to us. But this law has served them well for thousands of years and has avoided inbreeding and the genetic disaster that brings.'

She knew too well the damage a faulty gene could inflict. Picking up a fallen palm leaf, she fanned herself. 'The separate men and women's entrances to the clinic are a great idea. It must have been a lot harder to deliver culturally appropriate health care when you only had one waiting room and one examination room.'

His keen gaze suddenly intensified, hooking with hers as if he was seeing her for the very first time. Seeing her as herself rather than a RAN.

A shimmer of wondrous pleasure streaked through her, immediately chased by thundering unease. *Remember, no man can be a part of your life.*

Flynn pulled his hat off his head, breaking the moment. 'You're right about the old clinic. It was tough and we were fortunate to have a consultative approach when designing the new building.'

Susie, the health worker, came over. 'You two can't sit down yet. Time for you to become Kirri for a bit.'

Flynn laughed at Mia's confused look. 'Face painting.'

'Oh, right.' Mia rose to her feet and followed the health-care worker back to the group. 'So, Susie, what colour group do I get to wear?'

'Sun, fish, rock and pandanus. I'll give you all the colours.' Susie peeled layers from a reed until she found the firm centre. With experienced fingers she frayed the end until it acted like a brush. She made three brushes and put a circle of dots, yellow, red, white and black, across Mia's forehead, down her cheeks and across her chin.

'Smile.'

Mia glanced over and saw Flynn holding a small digital camera.

'The relatives down south will want to see this.'

She gave a tight smile. He was being thoughtful and she didn't want to break the moment by telling him there was no one down south, and she was the only person left in her family.

'Now you can go sit.' Susie instructed, and pointed to where Mia should go.

'Thanks, Susie.' She walked fifty metres and sat down again.

Flynn bent down next to her, his breath caressing her ear. With a mighty effort she held her head erect despite the temptation to lean toward him.

He spoke quietly so only she could hear. 'Take your hat off so the bad spirits can leave you.'

Bad spirits? Her breath caught in her throat. Surely he couldn't know what lurked inside her? She pulled the hat into her lap.

Susie approached her, holding smoking green leaves from the ironwood tree. Waving them over Mia's head, she chanted in Kirri, touching her head and her shoulders firmly with her hands.

Mia closed her eyes, letting the smoke waft around her, desperately wanting to believe that the smouldering leaves and a foreign language could remove from her the illness that dogged her family. The illness that had taken her mother and brother from her.

Knowing full well it would have no effect at all.

She breathed in long, slow breaths, pushing away the thoughts that permanently hovered close by, and willed herself to focus on the here and now. She tried to take life one day at a time and grasp every opportunity that came her way, but it wasn't always easy.

Opening her eyes, she looked around as fifteen dancers with their dark skins decorated moved in front of her, swaying to the beat of the clapping sticks.

'Crocodile dance, Mia.' Walter led a group of men in their dreaming dance, followed by a group of children.

'Rainbow Serpent dance!' Susie enthusiastically stamped her feet with her arms outstretched.

'This is amazing.' Mia's throat tightened as each group danced for her, showing their thanks.

'It's pretty special, isn't it?' Flynn's voice had a reverent quality to it that she'd not heard before.

Walter stopped in front of them. 'Flynn, you do the turtle dance, turtle man.'

Mia's head snapped around. 'Turtle man?'

Flynn shrugged his shoulders. 'It's a long story.' He lurched to his feet, his face creased in a huge smile and he joined the dancing throng.

White skin flashed pale against the black but the dance didn't differentiate colour. It accepted whoever chose to honour it. Voices merged as the song soared into the hot air, the joy of the dance evident on everyone's faces.

Mia couldn't help it, her eyes zeroed in on Flynn, so

much a part of this group. How many sides were there to this man? Doctor, pilot, teacher, advocate and now 'turtle man'.

Flynn came toward her, stamping his feet, waving his arms, his black stubbled cheeks giving him the look of a powerful warrior. Her heart pounded hard and fast, but she felt no fear from the man, only fear for herself as need and longing swirled inside her.

He stood above her tall and commanding. 'Come on, Walter and I will teach you the whirlwind dance.'

She shaded her eyes from the sun so she could see his face. 'Why the whirlwind dance?'

Walter laughed. 'Because since you've come to Kirra you've been a whirlwind.' He danced away, showing her the moves.

Flynn's large suntanned hands hovered in front of her, emanating strength, with tendons flexed and ready to pull her to her feet.

She hesitated, knowing she should rise from the earth on her own, but the temptation to touch him overwhelmed her and she slid her hands into his. These were not soft-palmed city hands. Yet his calloused grip closed over her with a tenderness she hadn't expected. Tantalising heat whirled through her, easily stripping away her intentions of only thinking about Flynn in terms of a doctor and teacher.

She gazed straight up at him and the noise of the dance receded as she lost herself in golden brown eyes the colour of maple syrup.

The moment drew out—his hands still holding hers, his heat flitting along her veins, both intoxicating and energising. With a firm but gentle tug, she rose to her feet, her mind and body spinning with newly discovered need.

Finally she found her voice. 'Thank you.'

An unusual huskiness clung to the words as he let go of her hands. 'No problem.'

Yes, big problem.

It was impossible to feel cold on Kirra but her palms ached with an unfamiliar chill. She instinctively clapped her hands together, joining Walter in the dance. Dancing the whirlwind to gain control.

Dancing the whirlwind to lock down the maelstrom of emotions that one brief look and touch from Flynn could unleash.

Dancing to forget.

CHAPTER FOUR

THE short flight between islands had been uneventful in the glorious conditions of late-afternoon winter sunshine. It didn't matter how many times he flew, Flynn never lost the feeling of complete awe when he caught site of Kirra. Ringed by aquamarine sea, edged by red and white sand, and dominated by the lush green of the canopy of trees, its naturally occurring tearshape looked like paradise.

Pity about the crocodiles, mantra rays and the snakes.

He lined the plane up with the Kirra airstrip and brought the Cessna down easily, thankful there were no gusting crosswinds. They'd come soon enough as the wet season approached. The moment the front wheels bounced on the tarmac, he opened the window to let in a breeze because the tiny plane was like a hotbox once it was on the ground.

He taxied down toward the gate, catching sight of the clinic ute barrelling along the gravel road in front of him, a plume of dust streaming out behind it. A honey-tanned arm waved to him.

Mia.

For the last few days he'd been busy running clinics

on the other islands. Usually his mind was completely focussed on the place he was working on, dealing with that community's issues, and giving scant thought to the other islands. But during the few quiet times on Mugur and Barra his mind had wandered back to Kirra and the ceremony. Back to Mia.

Back to the touch of Mia's hands in his. Back to the flickering shadows in her eyes. Back to the way she'd given herself up to the whirlwind dance as if she'd been shedding part of her soul.

He'd watched her dance and deep inside him something had ached.

But he wasn't thinking about that.

Whatever had caused those shadows was *her* secret. Everyone who came this far north had secrets. He didn't want to know and he sure as hell wasn't going to ask. Asking questions meant involvement. Asking questions opened him up to having questions asked back so he didn't do that any more. Getting involved meant getting hurt so the only way he got involved in people's lives now, was as their doctor.

Mia's secrets belonged to her and he intended to let her keep them.

He turned off the ignition and logged his times in the logbook. Then he grabbed his backpack, locked the plane and walked around toward the gate.

Mia leaned against the low fence, her long, blonde hair blowing out behind her as she fanned herself with her hat.

Every nerve ending fired off a volley of hot and hard need that swooped through him, leaving no place untouched.

Her rigid stance of two weeks ago had completely vanished. Instead, an aura of relaxation shimmered around her. In the place of neat and fitted cargo shorts with a blouse tucked in at the waist, she wore a simple island print dress that fell from her shoulders, the green and blue intersecting lines giving way to a band of yellow and red turtles that hovered around her knees. Cut for comfort, designed for coolness, it should have hung like a sack.

But the oncoming breeze blew it against her, outlining pert breasts, a slim waist and toned thighs. A supple body designed for touching.

Don't go there. He started mentally reciting the names of the bones in the body, driving some blood back to his brain from the pool in his groin. By the time he reached her, he could make coherent conversation.

He raised his brows. 'You've gone native on me?'

She laughed, the shadows in her eyes lifting for a moment. 'I know it's not regulation uniform but a baby vomited all over me. I figured you'd prefer to share the truck with me in Susie's spare dress than in my uniform, which reeks of curdled milk.'

'You've got me pegged.' He grinned at her. 'It might not be uniform but it suits you.'

She gripped the dress by the side seams and held it out as she glanced down at the fabric as if she was looking at it for the first time. 'Really?'

'Really.' The word came out overly low despite his attempt at making it sound casual.

She flicked her gaze up, her eyes shimmering like the sea. A flash of yearning, a flare of naked need broke through the shadows for a moment before receding. His blood pounded.

Work, think of work. He spun around and walked briskly to the truck. 'Anything happen this week that I need to know about?'

Silence met his question. He turned to see Mia walking toward him, her hips swaying in response to her relaxed gait.

She'd found her island time.

She shot him a teasing look. 'You're city-wired today.'

Laughter rumbled from deep inside him as she used his own words against him. 'And you're acclimatising.'

She shrugged and gave him a self-deprecating grin. 'The whirlwind's been downgraded to a light breeze. Here, catch. I've been driving all day.' She tossed him the keys and hopped into the truck. 'I even gave up on the immunisation clinic idea. Instead I had a sausage sizzle and fruit festa and I ended up immunising more children than I had on my initial list.'

He swung up next to her. 'Good for you.' He couldn't get over the change in her. Not only was she more relaxed, she almost glowed with good health. Perhaps the shadows in her eyes had just been fatigue and not secrets after all. Not that he cared either way. He was just glad for her that after a few weeks away from the stress of city living she'd found her niche.

He turned the truck around and headed back toward town. 'So what's been happening?'

She tucked her hair back from her face. 'I'm still experimenting with the bread idea. Jimmy is my chief taste-tester.'

He caught a waft of her tropical perfume and gripped the wheel. 'How's his wound?'

'Healing really well. Do you want another set of liver-function tests and electrolytes just as a final round-up before he's officially discharged off the books?'

'That's probably a good idea considering the history of kidney disease on the island.' He had to concentrate on keeping his eyes on the road rather than snatching glances at Mia.

'Oh, and we had a brawl and I had to stitch a few people.'

Startled, he swung his head around so quickly his neck ricked. Her matter-of-fact tone almost implied she'd added that fact in as an afterthought.

Were you safe? His heart jumped as the unexpected thought rammed through him, pushing aside his usual and immediate need to know about the patients. Completely disconcerting him.

He tried to sound casual as he stared at the road. 'Was Robbo around?' The policeman had a large territory and he wasn't always in town when trouble broke out.

She twisted her hair up off her neck and slid in a wide comb to hold it in place. 'Yes, and he dealt with it all very quickly.'

Relief spread through him. 'Good.' The word came out crisp, clean and professional. The doctor in him was back in control and all was well in his world. 'Who was hurt?'

She crossed her legs, and her dress moved up, exposing a honey-tanned thigh.

He gripped the wheel more tightly.

Mia tugged at her hem. 'No one you would know.

Six young blokes from Brisbane flew in for a few days' fishing. They got into a fight with a couple of local lads over some women. I stitched them up, wrote a referral letter to their doctors and Robbo sent two of them back to Darwin and warned the others. It's all been very quiet since.'

He smiled at her. 'It sounds like you're well and truly finding your feet and you didn't miss me at all.'

What are you saying? He hadn't flirted with a woman in two years so why was he starting now?

'Actually, I did miss you.' The words vibrated deeply around the cab of the truck.

The wheels hit a pothole he'd been planning to miss. He snatched another look at her face, trying to match the statement with her expression.

Cornflower-blue eyes sparkled. 'I haven't had a decent cup of coffee since you left.' She touched a reddened area on the back of her hand. 'That coffee-machine of yours hates me and spits steam at me. I don't think I could have waited another day for you to get back because my lack of caffeine is giving me the shakes.'

A rush of lightness streaked through him and he had a crazy desire to hum. He grinned, enjoying her sense of humour. 'Forget all about saving lives, it's good to know I'm missed for something really important.'

'Coffee is important.' Her face dissolved into deep laughter lines in complete contrast to the serious tone of her voice, and she giggled like a young girl.

He laughed with her as warmth spread through him like a rising sun sending out its rays, slowly waking up parts of him that had slumbered for too long. This woman had more facets to her than a crystal.

Suddenly she gripped the doorhandle, her knuckles white. 'Stop the truck. Now!'

Her voice sharp and furious sliced through him and he instantly jammed on the brakes. 'What's wr—?'

But she'd jumped out of the still-moving truck and was running through the scrub, dodging cycads, their silver fronds glinting in the sun. He caught a flash of colour and realised that a Kirri teenager was pulling back away from a non-Kirri man whose hand tightly gripped her upper arm.

'Hey!' Mia's shout blew back to him on the wind.

The man swung around to face Mia, his balance unsteady, his expression surprised. His free hand held a shotgun.

Flynn saw the gun at the same moment the truck stopped. Fear for Mia's safety gripped the pit of his stomach as acid shot into it. Every muscle in his body tensed, ready to run, ready to fight, ready to knock Mia out of harm's way. But instinct overruled impulse. Accosting a man who held a gun and who looked high on an unknown substance would put Mia and the girl in more danger than they already were.

The man's grip must have loosened on the girl's arm at Mia's shout because she suddenly ducked and weaved behind Mia, before breaking into a run and disappearing into the bush.

Flynn's chest tightened as if a steel band had closed around his ribcage. How would the man react now the girl had fled? With his eyes glued to the scene he radioed the police.

As he slipped quietly out of the truck, Flynn heard Mia speak, her voice remarkably steady. 'I thought you were here to fish, Joel?'

Flynn realised this must be one of the fishing tourists.

Joel staggered toward Mia. 'That's right, sweetheart.' His slurred words tumbled over each other.

Mia stood perfectly still. 'This is a long way from the water and too close to town to hunt.' Her head inclined towards the gun.

Joel looked down at his hand as if the gun was something he wasn't expecting to be holding. 'I came in for some…' He scratched his head. 'Supplies.'

She kept her hands open and her arms hanging loosely by her sides. 'You're looking a bit hot and tired. I've got some water in the truck. Would you like a drink?'

That was Flynn's entrée into the situation. He grabbed the water bottles and walked slowly toward Mia and Joel, the bottles in front of him, clearly in view.

Joel's unfocussed gaze wandered from Mia to Flynn. 'Have you got any beer, mate?'

Now didn't seem the time to remind Joel it was illegal to have alcohol on Kirra except in the club. He adopted the conspiratorial tone of two blokes on a mission. 'I can take you into town for some.' He handed over a water bottle.

'Yeah? Good. At least I can go back to the boys with beer. The girl got away.' He leered at Mia and then rubbed his eyes as if that would help improve his focus.

Flynn caught the pinprick size of his pupils and wondered if he'd consumed more than just beer.

Tension lined Mia's face but her voice sounded

conversational. 'I'm boiling. Let's get into the cool of the truck.'

Placing himself firmly between Mia and Joel, Flynn made sure they all turned together, making their way back to the vehicle. 'So, have you caught any barramundi?' Flynn tried to sound as normal as possible, his eyes fixed on the gun.

But Joel remained silent, concentrating on the seemingly difficult task of putting one foot in front of the other.

Mia walked next to him, the scent of her fear mixing with her perfume. He knew how she felt. The unpredictability of the man made every moment like walking through a minefield, never knowing if or when the bomb would go off.

As they reached the truck, Flynn pointed to the gun box and prayed his gambit would work. 'I'll stow your gun in the back for safekeeping.' He could feel Mia's penetrating gaze behind him and he knew exactly what the target was.

Joel's brow furrowed as he processed the statement. He slowly raised the gun, his hand close to the trigger.

Flynn held his breath, not daring to look away from Joel. Wanting desperately to look at Mia.

'There you go, mate.' Joel pushed the gun into his hands.

'Thanks.' Flynn locked his knees against the desire to sag against the truck. He immediately uncocked the gun, checking for ammunition before laying it in the gun box. A red cartridge full of shot lay inside the barrel. His gut churned acid into his throat at what might have been.

The roar of an engine made them all turn. A white four-wheel-drive police vehicle pulled up next to them. Robbo hopped out. 'Need a hand, Flynn?'

Relief flooded him. 'That would be great. I've got a customer for you. And I think you might want to talk to Lizzie Wonterrgerra later to see if she wants to lay a complaint about this man.'

Five minutes later Robbo drove back to town with Joel in the back of the vehicle. Flynn had promised to call by the police lockup and do a physical examination before Joel and his mates were put on a plane back to the mainland.

Running his hand through his hair, he turned to Mia, his fear finally finding voice. 'What possessed you to run into a potentially violent situation? You could have been killed!'

She pursed her lips and crossed her arms over her chest. 'But I wasn't. Besides, when your number's up, it's up.' She tossed her head, and her hair tumbled from its comb, cascading across her shoulders. 'Obviously it wasn't my time.'

'Your time?' He tried unsuccessfully to keep his voice level at this fey belief. 'But that's crazy thinking. You don't willingly put yourself into dangerous situations and say it's fate.'

'I didn't know he had a gun.' Her eyes shone overly bright as her hands balled into tight fists by her side. 'Anyway, if you'd seen him pulling that girl you would have done the same thing. I acted on instinct.'

He couldn't make her out. Her reaction defied all logic. 'No, you acted on *impulse*, and they're two completely different things. Impulse is without thought. Your brain processes them differently.'

She immediately stilled and stared at him, panic suddenly flaring in her eyes, the shadows that dogged her reappearing.

What the hell was going on?

Her face drained of colour, her rosy cheeks fading to white on white, and her entire body started to shudder.

Shock.

Damn it. In a heartbeat she'd gone from shrugging off facing down a man with a gun into shock. He grabbed a blanket from the truck, quickly wrapping it around her trembling shoulders and pulled her close.

Getting involved as a doctor. Giving a patient support.

His arms tightened around her, his body absorbing her tremors. Absorbing her heat.

Her tremors subsided.

The doctor would step back now.

But her warmth rolled through him, sparking a slow, burning heat. Heat that built in intensity, generating an undeniable need. A need that kept her in his arms.

Her head rested under his chin, the silky strands of her hair soft against his skin. Her sweet scent tickled his nostrils, tempting him.

He lowered his face into her hair, breathing deeply, inhaling the complex aroma that was Mia. He stroked her hair, tucking stray strands behind her ear. 'Hell, Mia, you gave me a fright.'

'I didn't mean to put you in danger.' She slowly raised her head, and brought her hand to his cheek, her fingers stroking with a feather-light touch. 'I'm sorry.'

Jolts of need, like sparks of electricity, zigzagged through his body. He looked down into eyes wide with contrition, backlit with tangled and swirling emotions. He recognised need.

Her head tilted upward, and her lush bottom lip quivered, calling to him.

Two weeks of self-control vanished. He stifled a groan and lowered his mouth.

His lips touched hers and his mind blanked to everything except the touch of her mouth against his. Soft, pliant lips that tasted of bush plums and adrenaline. Lips that grazed and stroked his, the lightest touch sending spirals of pure need, white and hot ripping through him.

His hand curled gently around the back of her neck, his fingers tangling in her hair, wanting to hold her against him, have her mouth melded to his.

All space between them vanished. He swallowed her moan as her body pressed against his, the cotton dress too thin to be any real barrier. Her arms rose and ringed his neck, pushing her breasts hard against his chest, and her thighs tensed against his own.

He sought to deepen the kiss, to plunder her mouth, to take what his body craved so badly. His tongue flicked against her lips.

For an infinitesimal moment, Mia sagged against him, opening her mouth to his and giving.

The gift stunned him with its intensity.

And then she pulled back and it was gone.

How could you miss something you'd barely had?

* * *

Using every ounce of strength, Mia stepped back out of Flynn's embrace. Away from his lips, which had scorched the flimsy barricades she'd put up to protect herself from him. Away from his warmth and his comfort. Away from his heartbeat, which had pounded against her chest, regular and strong, his life force transferring itself to her, making her body respond in ways that would only bring her more heartache.

You acted on impulse. Impulse is without thought. His words pummelled her, their accuracy piercing. Memories of her mother's legendary shopping trips flooded her—impulse buying on a grand scale. Sixty-three CDs in half an hour, the three cars she'd bought one Saturday afternoon because she hadn't been able to decide on the colour and the scarfs she'd shoplifted. All of them had been signs. The start of her mother's decline, the start of her dementia.

You're twenty-six. Mia rallied her common sense, reminding herself that her mother had almost been forty when her first symptoms had appeared.

'Mia?' Flynn's husky voice broke into her thoughts. 'You've gone pale again.' His eyes narrowed. 'What's going on?'

Panic fluttered in her gut. She didn't talk about her mother. Not to anyone. She had to deflect him. 'Nothing's going on. Well, obviously not nothing.' She wrung her hands, words pouring from her mouth in a gabble. 'I mean there was Joel, the gun, and I kissed you.' She shrugged. 'Sorry about that, blame the shock. It won't happen again. I mean, I'm the RAN, you're the doctor and—'

'You don't have to apologise.' His voice had a cool

edge to it despite his seemingly understanding smile. 'These things happen during stressful situations. Come on, I'll take you home.'

She nodded. 'Thanks.' She should feel relieved that the kiss had been talked about, dealt with and dismantled. But the remnants of it still lingered in her body, not so easily dismissed.

The amazing red cliffs of the coast road provided enough conversation to ease the tension and attempt to return things to normal. Whatever normal was because every time she was with Flynn normality seemed to tip on its head.

Kissing him! Had she no sense at all? Hadn't she learned a single thing from Steven?

Once she was home she would soak in a bath and forget the last hour. Forget Joel, the gun and Flynn's kiss. Lose them all in a sea of bubbles.

The truck pulled up, parking under a riot of purple bougainvillea. Mia unlatched her seat belt and turned to Flynn, planning to exit the truck as the RAN, *not* the woman who had melted against him when his lips had stroked her own. 'I've left a stack of blood results on your desk for your signature. There's nothing urgent.'

'They can wait until tomorrow.'

She nodded slowly. 'OK, see you tomorrow then.' She pulled the doorhandle and hopped out of the vehicle, breathing out a long, slow breath of relief. They'd restored professionalism and tomorrow it would be like the kiss had never happened.

But right now she needed a cup of tea, a long, cool bath and then to watch a chick-flick DVD with a packet of chocolate biscuits that she'd been saving for emergencies. She walked to the back of the truck to get her bag.

Flynn beat her to it. He casually picked it up and walked up her front steps, stopping in front of her door, his feet firmly planted on her veranda. His handsome face wore a determined expression.

Her heart hammered wildly. Why had he got out of the truck? She put out her hand to accept the backpack. 'Thanks for that. Don't you need to get down to the police station?'

He raised his brows. 'Robbo will ring when he's ready for me. Meanwhile, you've been in shock and I'm coming in to make sure you eat and drink something.'

Alarm bells rang shrilly and she went into damage control. She didn't want him to come inside, have him in her small house, filling the space with his charisma and charm. Tempting her. 'That's really kind of you but I'm fine now.'

He stood implacable and unmoving. 'I'm the doctor and I don't think you're fine at all.' His clear gaze penetrated down to her soul. 'I think whatever it is that you're running away from caught up with you today.'

Blood roared in her ears as her stomach dropped. She wanted to deny it but her voice stuck in her throat.

He plucked the key from of her lifeless fingers and pushed it into the lock. 'And I think it's time you talked about it.'

CHAPTER FIVE

FLYNN hummed as he pan-fried kangaroo in Mia's well-stocked kitchen. He suddenly realised how much he missed cooking. When he was on Mugur and Barra different families took it in turns to invite him to eat with them. Just recently he'd been so busy on Kirra that he'd missed the deadline for ordering food and when he'd cooked for himself his meals had been pretty basic, drawing on his stock of emergency tinned food.

But Mia had a pantry that made cooking a joy. He heard the shuddering of the water hammer and then the gentle fall of the shower. Mia had insisted he did not need to stay and had retreated to the bathroom. He was banking on the tantalising aroma of Asian spices to smoke her out. He tossed the capsicum and onions into the wok on the other burner and wondered if Mia had any wine.

What are you doing? The protective voice that had been part of him for two years roared in his head as an image of cooking for Brooke in their shared kitchen sucked the breath from his lungs.

No, this was *nothing* like that. This meal was medicinal. He dumped the Hokkien noodles into the wok, forking them free of each other. He couldn't move past Mia saying, 'When your number's up, it's up.' It was at odds with the thoroughness he saw in her work—the note-keeping—as if she was determined to get everything right. The two things clashed, making little sense. *That* was the only reason he'd broken his vow of never asking people why they came to Kirra. As her colleague, he needed to understand.

Understand and keep her safe.

He banged the spatula hard against the side of the wok, the sound of metal against metal ringing in his head, driving out the unwanted words. He didn't need to keep her safe. Not Mia or any other woman. Women rejected his care. First his mother, then Brooke.

'That smells good.' Mia appeared and walked straight to the cutlery drawer, pulling out forks and spoons. Tendrils of damp hair curled around her cheeks, having escaped from the confines of her damp French braid. She looked fresh, clean and sexy.

The vivid memory of her lips against his thudded through him. He snapped off the small gas stove with more force than necessary. 'If you grab the sweet chilli sauce from the fridge, I'll serve up.'

'Done.' She smiled and opened the fridge door.

With an almost magnetic pull his gaze strayed to her as she leaned forward, reaching into the back of the fridge. Her vest top rose to reveal an expanse of smooth, golden skin. Skin that screamed to be touched, caressed and tasted.

Concentrate. He was here to eat, talk, learn and leave. He filled two large bowls with the steaming concoction and placed them on earthy-coloured, woven pandanus placemats.

Mia sat down opposite him and poured icy-cold water into tumblers. The tension that was so much a part of her almost audibly buzzed like electricity.

He needed her to relax. He tapped the mats. 'Have you been out to the women's workshop to see these being made?'

She nodded, her jaw stiff and her slender neck rigid. 'I went out the other day and Ruby showed me how they boil the pandanus with different roots to get the colours. I couldn't believe it when she pulled up this spindly, half-dead-looking plant and the root was a vivid red.'

'Tassie's verdant green must make this place look like another planet.' He smiled and wound the noodles around his fork. 'Did you grow up in Tasmania?'

'I did.' She put a spoonful of food in her mouth as her eyes flashed him a challenging look. With a full mouth she couldn't talk.

First the shower, now the food. She had delaying tactics down to an art form. He sipped his water and waited, hoping Robbo didn't choose right then to call him.

'And where did you grow up, Flynn?' Her voice sounded strained.

Two could play at this game. 'Brisbane.' He filled his mouth with food and winked at her.

She coughed and reached for her water.

They ate in relative silence, as if a truce had been called so they could enjoy the meal. The only sound being heard was the *uk uk uk* song of the frogs.

Mia finally emptied her bowl. 'Thank you, that was

the best meal I've had since arriving.' Her smile softened the strained politeness.

'You're welcome. I haven't cooked in a while so it felt good to be back in a kitchen.' He finished his final mouthful and put down his fork, deciding to push the issue. 'I know you don't want to tell me, but talking can help.'

Mia moved her bowl to the side and fiddled with the edge of the placemat. 'Have you noticed that the people who say that aren't the ones baring their souls?'

He thought back to when Brooke had left. 'Perhaps they've been there before you and have learned the value.'

Her gaze flicked over him. 'You're not going to leave until I tell you, are you?'

He grinned, trying to take the edge off the tense situation. 'No.'

She pushed her chair back, the legs screeching against the lino. 'What can I say? It's been a bad twelve months.'

'I'm sorry to hear it. Some years are better than others.' He knew that only too well.

'Yeah.' She stood up and took the bowls into the kitchen.

Every part of him wanted to stand up and follow her but he stayed put. She needed some space. *You need the space.*

He also needed to understand. 'And this bad year makes you believe that life is just directed by fate?'

She stilled at the sink and then turned slowly, her eyes chillingly empty of emotion. 'Why not believe that? Who has control over what happens? I sure don't.'

The harshness of her words tinged with her pain hit him like a blow to the chest. He spoke quietly, trying to be the voice of reason in an emotional whirlpool. 'We all have some control. We have choices, we make decisions that—'

Her strained voice cut across his. 'My mother and brother died this year. I sure as hell didn't choose for that to happen.' She reached for a packet of chocolate biscuits, ripping the package open and slamming it onto the bench. 'Just like I didn't choose for my father to drop dead of a heart attack when I was sixteen. If I could control things, then none of that would have happened and I would still have a family.'

Defiantly, she crossed her arms and tilted her chin. 'So, yes, sue me for not being scientific like you but I think fate plays a big role in my life.'

Her words rained down on him like a flood of pain and circled his heart, lapping at his professional distance. He gripped the edge of the table to keep himself seated. To keep him from going to her and hauling her back into his arms, and stroking away her grief.

To keep himself safe.

Safe from making the same mistake again with a woman.

Mia bit her lip and stared at Flynn, her heart thudding hard against her ribs. Would he stop there? Would he accept her explanation and not ask how or why her mother and Michael had died? Accept that grief had made her act so foolishly today? She hardly dared breathe.

'Mia, you're right, you've had a bad year and I'm sorry. I wouldn't wish that on anyone.' He rose slowly

to his feet, his face full of empathy but tinged with
steely determination. 'But…'

The tiny word hung in the air, its sound always
ominous. She swallowed hard and kept her gaze on
him, as if staring him down would stop him asking any
more questions.

He cleared his throat. 'But as much as you miss them,
you have your life to live. They'd want you to grab hold
of every day and live it to the full, without taking stupid
risks that could end it all too early.'

It's going to end up that way no matter what I do. She
bit off the words that roared in her head and pushed
them down, refusing to think about them. 'Thank you,
I'll keep that in mind.'

A muscle twitched in his neck as his forehead
creased in a frown. She glimpsed a flash of something
in his eyes that said her laid-back doctor wasn't so at
peace with the world as he wanted everyone to believe.

He opened his mouth to speak but the shrill ring of
his phone interrupted.

She spoke first. 'That's Robbo, right?'

He checked the display and nodded. 'I have to go.'
His eyes, full of concern, caught hers. 'Will you be OK?'

Please, stop being so caring, it's all too hard to resist.
She walked him to the door. 'I'm fine.'

He hesitated at the threshold. 'Mia…'

She put her hand on his back, her fingers meeting taut
muscle and corded tendons. 'Go.' She pushed him
gently out the door, her fingers wanting desperately to
grip his shoulder and haul him back.

* * *

Mia pulled into the clinic car park half an hour later than expected, dreaming about a cool shower followed by a tall iced drink of soda water and lemon. But she knew that the daydream was as close as she was going to get to either of them for a few hours. Although it was Saturday, she was behind in the stock take and ordering, and if she was to have the drugs she needed come Monday, she had to fax the order to Darwin today. Then she had to mow the clinic grass, grab a shower and be at the church by four for Susie's eldest daughter's wedding.

She glanced down, grimacing at the mess that was her clothes and was thankful it was Saturday and no one was around. She ducked into the staff entrance. Flynn wasn't due in for an hour, not that time meant anything to him but she could be pretty certain that he wouldn't be early. The second clinic truck was still parked so his plane hadn't landed.

She pulled open the door, crossed the threshold and walked straight into a solid wall of muscle.

Flynn.

Her hand shot out and gripped his upper arm, as much to stop her knees from buckling as to steady herself.

'Hello.' His smiling greeting vibrated with deep laughter as his keen hazel gaze roved lazily from the top of her head to the tips of her toes. 'You've been having some fun, lying around. When did you dye your hair red?'

Mini-explosions of heat detonated inside her as his stare touched and torched every part of her. Every red-dust-covered part. Heat morphed into a fire of longing which streaked through her, pooling deep inside her, stalling her brain and reducing her leg muscles to quivering jelly.

'Someone took the tarpaulin out of the truck and I had to change a flat tyre out on the Bathurst road. The only way I could get to the spare tyre was to crawl under the truck.' She tossed her dust-impregnated hair in her best attempt at a haughty look, but her lips twitched in a smile. 'Only a man could decide it was a great idea to put a spare tyre under a car where it gets covered in filth.'

Dimples carved into the dark stubble on his cheeks. 'At least it isn't the wet season, although they tell me mud is great for the skin.' His voice dropped to a low rumble. 'People pay to get covered in the stuff.' He leaned forward and pulled a twig from her hair, his fingers gently brushing her scalp.

White lights flickered in front of her eyes and an image of Flynn, naked and covered in mud, stole all coherent thought. Somehow she made her feet step back, away from his aura, away from his scent of sunshine and soap, and away from temptation.

'I'm off to mow the grass so I'm just going to wash off a bit of dust so I can put on sunscreen.'

He grinned. 'Oh I don't know, the locals will just think you're ready for a ceremony and you overdid it on the red.'

She put her hands on her hips in mock indignation. 'Ha-ha, very funny, turtle man. I believe the indigenous ceremony is tomorrow after the church service.'

His easygoing grin slid off his face and his cheekbones suddenly seemed stark and pointed, giving him a hard look. 'What church service?'

She couldn't hide the disbelief in her voice and she knew her expression must be one of stupefaction. 'Susie's daughter's wedding.' She threw up her hands. 'I swear blokes just tune out. How could you have forgotten? It's all Susie's been talking for the last few weeks. That's why you're back this weekend, right, instead of being on Barra?'

A muscle twitched in his neck and then he smiled, although it didn't quite reach his eyes. 'That's right, it's at four o'clock. I was just testing you.'

Testing she'd remembered? A spasm of fear gripped her before her rational brain overruled it. No, surely not. He had no idea about her mother and inherited fronto-temporal dementia. He was probably just covering for his own memory lapse.

'You better get going, then, if you want to beat the bride to the church.' The words came out crisp and efficient before he turned and walked down the corridor.

She made her way into the bathroom, her brain buzzing. What was that all about? One minute he was flirting with her and the next he'd closed down. Perhaps he'd been embarrassed that he'd forgotten the wedding? She wouldn't have thought that would have embarrassed him but, then again, she didn't really know what made him tick.

But she knew he made her body quiver with longing.

A couple of weeks had passed since Flynn had cooked her dinner. *Since he held you in his arms.* She sighed against the thought she'd tried so hard to let go of, but couldn't. Her dreams were full of Flynn—his firm arms around her, his taut body against her, his lips seeking her lips—and she woke up hot, bothered and aching with unfulfilled need for him.

She loved and hated the dreams in equal measure.

She quickly filled the basin with warm water and pumped soap into her hands, squishing it between her fingers. Flynn flew in and out of her life and had in a few weeks turned it completely upside down. She loved being a RAN on Kirra. It was everything she needed and wanted—remote and working solo having been the key attractions. But when Flynn was on the other islands she found herself counting the days until he returned to Kirra.

His arrival always generated a lightness inside her, a sense of anticipation and excitement that she'd never expected to experience again. He brought a shining light into the darkness that had been her past year. She craved that lightness. She craved him.

He gave you comfort, that was all. His arms around her after the incident with Joel had been the act of a caring man, a colleague and perhaps a friend. And that was all it could ever be because she was a walking time bomb and no man wanted her. Steven had been proof of that.

She sloshed water onto her face and up her arms, and watched the dust turn it the colour of rust. She stared into the mirror as rivulets of water left streaky marks on her face. Flynn hadn't tried to kiss her again. Since that night he'd been nothing more than a colleague.

She reminded herself that this was a good thing and she should just accept it and move on. But her thoughts kept returning to the glimpse of hurt she'd seen in his eyes just before he'd gone to the police station.

He kept his own counsel. She realised that he'd never

mentioned his family and he didn't take off to Darwin once a month like most of the other non-indigenous community workers did to meet their girlfriends, boy-friends, wives and family.

And yet he was very much a part of the Kirra commu-nity, well respected and loved. He coached the kids in footy, he was 'turtle man'. He belonged in so many ways.

Her first image of him as a maverick crocodile hunter, a stand-alone guy, clashed with the caring doctor and the enthusiastic community member she'd got to know. Good men like Flynn were usually married with adoring wives and gorgeous children.

So why wasn't he?

'Mia, I need a hand.' Flynn's voice called her name from the treatment room.

She grabbed a towel, dried her face and hands, pulled a patient gown over her filthy clothes and went back to work.

'We'll have you feeling better soon.' Flynn tousled the hair of nine-year-old Alice and kept a smile on his face as he inwardly sighed. He could have her feeling better soon but making her better was a different thing entirely.

The sick young girl looked at him forlornly as she lay on the examination couch, her knees up under her chin.

'What's up?'

He glanced up as Mia walked into the room, her face scrubbed clean of outback dust and her cheeks pink with good health. The familiar rush streaked through him, the one he got every time he saw her, even when she was filthy and bedraggled. Dirt couldn't dim her innate beauty and neither had her grief.

It was a tough gig, losing your family in one go. He assumed it had been a car accident. But despite her loss she still managed to glow with a life-affirming energy and it radiated from her eyes, her mouth, the sway of her hips…

He ran his hand through his hair. He'd been convinced he could shut out his attraction but Mia had moved into his mind, taken up residence in his thoughts and dreams, and despite numerous resolutions to move her out he'd been pathetically unsuccessful. He'd resisted beautiful women before but Mia was different. Strength and vulnerability—he found the combination captivating.

But it had to stop.

He'd hated it that he'd flown back to spend the weekend on Kirra because of Mia, completely forgetting about Susie's daughter's wedding. Had his mind been more focussed he would have stayed on Barra this weekend, like he'd originally planned.

It was a lapse like this that really drove home that the time had come for life to go back to normal, to the uncomplicated way it had been before Mia had arrived.

And it started now with a teaching session. The moment that was over, he'd create a reason to fly to Barra. No way was he going to stay on Kirra for the wedding.

He beckoned Mia forward with his hand. 'I want you to examine Alice and tell me what you think she has.'

Mia's large blue eyes blinked in puzzlement. 'Is this a test? Something you're expecting me not to know?'

He grimaced. 'There's every chance you won't have seen this down south.'

'Is her mother with her?'

'No. Her uncle brought her in and he's outside.'

'And he won't be able to come in.' Understanding washed across her face and she walked over to a cupboard and pulled out a worn teddy bear in green scrubs. Then she returned to their patient. 'I'm Mia, Alice, and I'm going to have a look at you. Would you like to hold my doctor bear while I do it?'

Alice stared and then extended her chubby hand, grabbing the bear and clutching it tightly to her chest.

As Flynn expected, Mia started by taking the child's temperature with the ear thermometer.

'It's high. Thirty nine point four.' She immediately recorded it on the chart. She then examined Alice's glands, and checked for eye and nose discharge. Turning to Flynn, she said, 'There's some evidence of nosebleeds.'

Flynn nodded. 'Every sign builds a diagnosis.'

Mia returned her attention to her patient. 'Alice, I need you to say, "Ah."'

Alice stared at her.

Mia glanced at Flynn.

'Alice is from the north of the island and very little English is spoken.' Flynn pulled out a chair and sat astride it to watch how Mia would handle this.

Mia tapped Alice on the shoulder and then tapped her own shoulder and said, 'Ahh.'

The girl obediently opened her mouth and Mia, using a tongue depressor and a pen torch, examined her tonsils.

A deep furrow appeared on Mia's forehead as she dropped the tongue depressor into the bin. She studied the girl's face very carefully. 'I think she has a twitch or it could just be her being stressed by being here.'

Flynn nodded, deliberately noncommittal.

Horizontal lines crinkled across the bridge of her nose and suddenly she screwed up her face and said, 'Ouch, ooh,' and patted down her own body.

Alice nodded and pointed to her ankles, her knees and her elbows and then her stomach.

Mia laid her down with the teddy and tucked a sheet around her middle, leaving her arms and legs exposed. She started to examine the girl's limbs. 'I can feel raised bumps in clusters on her joints which move.' She flicked on the light and peered carefully. 'She also has scabies.'

Flynn smiled. 'Well spotted.' He saw Mia's shoulders relax slightly. He knew she'd feel like this was an exam but it was really important she could diagnose this condition.

'Her joints are all swollen. It could be rheumatoid arthritis.'

'It could be.' Flynn deliberately gave no hints.

Mia's short, abrupt laugh sounded stressed. 'This is as bad as my final exams.'

'You're doing fine.'

'But I know I haven't nailed it yet.' Mia shot him a smile—a mixture of determination and challenge with a spark of something he knew was just for him.

A picture thudded into his mind of Mia lying next to him, her eyes shining with laughter and lust. His blood immediately pounded hard and fast and he breathed out slowly, filling his mind with every reason why he couldn't act on this attraction. His body ignored him.

Mia sat Alice up and showed her the stethoscope and then listened to her heart. 'I can hear a diastolic murmur.'

She was getting close but he'd seen doctors get it wrong.

Mia stroked Alice's hair and then she came and sat down next to Flynn, her eyes perceptive and keen. 'Does she have rheumatic fever?'

He nodded slowly. 'She does. You did well.'

She half smiled and half grimaced, as if making the correct diagnosis was, in fact, the wrong thing.

He understood how she felt. Sometimes being right didn't give you a buzz of satisfaction.

Mia bit her lip. 'You're right, I've never seen it before. Mind you, I hadn't seen too much scabies either, although down south the kids all seem to get molluscum contagiosum.' She glanced back to Alice, who clutched her bear close. 'Poor little thing, no wonder she's feeling so sick.'

He rubbed his chin. 'Current thinking is that scabies is the cause.'

Mia started. 'But I thought rheumatic fever followed a strep throat infection. How do skin mites fit into the picture?'

He leaned forward, enjoying having such an enthusiastic student. 'Untreated scabies causes skin infections and streptococcus is the culprit. Alice has scabies and her body is busy fighting the strep bacteria, but certain body tissues are similar so we get antibodies fighting heart values and joints.'

Mia nodded, following his line of thought. 'And that's rheumatic fever.'

'Yes, but the strep also causes glomerulonephritis, which leads to kidney disease.'

Understanding crossed her face. 'I wondered why there seemed to be such a high rate of kidney problems here. I don't suppose all those dogs help.'

'Actually, the dogs are in the clear. Mange is caused by a different mite altogether and doesn't cause human scabies.' He stood up and walked over to Alice. 'Skin disease is also linked to high rates of gastroenteritis and pneumonia in kids. Their bodies are so busy fighting the skin infection, they have no reserves left to fight other bugs.'

Mia's blue eyes shimmered as the reality of poverty and overcrowding hit home. 'So next week I get creative on how to tackle the scabies problem.'

Her compassion and caring wafted over him and for a brief moment he wondered what it would be like to have her care for him.

Every protective barrier shot back into place with a loud clang. *Women don't care for you. They leave you when you love them.*

'So what's the treatment plan for Alice?'

Mia's question broke into his thoughts, grounding him. Giving him a perfect reason to leave Kirra today and avoid the wedding. 'Good old penicillin, and ongoing treatment with antibiotics. She'll need an echo-cardiogram, an ECG and a full blood examination, as well as bed rest. I'll take her to Darwin.'

Mia's pen paused over her notebook and she stared straight at him, confusion darkening her eyes. 'But we can do all that here except the echocardiogram.'

'Which is why I'll take her to Darwin.' The words rushed out brusque and snappy.

She raised her brows and walked over to a list pinned up on the wall, trailing her long, slender fingers down the paper, pausing halfway down. 'The cardiologist is due here for his bimonthly visit on Friday and it clearly says, "Echo clinic."'

She spun back to face him, a conspiratorial smile flitting across her cheeks. 'I can sweet-talk the appointments clerk into accepting Alice, and as you say over and over, if we don't have to evacuate a patient so much the better. And that way you won't miss Susie's daughter's wedding.' Her expression was one of 'situation sorted'. 'I'll get the penicillin injection.'

His chest tightened as if bands of steel circled his torso. 'Patient care is far more important than attending a wedding. She needs bed rest and I'm taking her to Darwin today.'

Mia's gaze immediately narrowed, zeroing in on his face with uncompromising intensity. 'Of course patient care comes ahead of a wedding.'

'I'm glad we're on the same page.' He breathed out, not realising he'd been holding his breath. 'You can go to the wedding and represent the clinic and I'll take Alice to Darwin.'

'I don't think so.' She tossed her head and a fine layer of red dust floated around her, looking like a halo. 'This treatment plan goes against everything you've ever taught me. It goes against everything you believe. She's sick but not as critical as Jimmy, and you kept him here.'

Her words rained down on him, their truth harsh

and accurate. 'I believe I'm the doctor, Mia, and I make the final decisions about patients in my care.'

Mia folded her arms across her chest, her eyes glinting like sparks from a welding iron. *'Primum non nocere.'*

First do no harm. The Hippocratic oath.

Anger simmered inside him, as much against himself as Mia. 'What about it?' He strode over to the desk, planning on ringing Royal Darwin Hospital. Alice would benefit from some good food and real rest in hospital.

'I want to know the *real* reason why you're evaccing a non-critical patient on a Saturday afternoon.'

The walls of the clinic seemed to close in on him. He had to deflect her, make her stop. 'I don't have to justify my medical decisions to you. I'm the doctor, you're only the RAN.'

She flinched, the tremor running along her jaw and down through her body, but she held her ground. 'You do have to justify your decisions if they're coloured by something personal.'

He dropped the phone back in the handset as her soft words pierced him. He turned to look at Alice, whose eyes were wide with confusion, not understanding what was going on. He rubbed the back of his neck. Hell, what was he doing? He couldn't take her to Darwin. Mia was right. He couldn't let his personal feelings affect his medical judgement.

He raised his gaze to Mia's—a gaze full of steely determination and concern. Concern for him—despite the cruel barb he'd just sent her way.

He didn't want to see concern or pity in her eyes. That had been why he'd left Brisbane. 'Alice will stay here.'

'Good.' She smiled at him as if he was a recalcitrant child finally doing the right thing. 'I'll organise for Jenny to come and sit with Alice.'

There was no way he was going to that wedding. 'No need to do that. I'll stay.'

She shook her head vehemently. 'You're not needed here. You're the island's doctor and that comes with responsibilities other than just treating patients. You're going to support one of our most experienced health workers by attending the wedding of her daughter.' Her eyes flashed as her hands gripped her hips. 'We will get Alice settled and Jenny installed. Then, before we go to the church, you're going to tell me what on earth is going on.'

Right then he realised he'd lost the battle. After two years on the run his past had finally caught up with him and he had nowhere left to hide.

CHAPTER SIX

'ALICE'S temperature has come down and she's asleep.' Mia poured a large glass of cold mineral water and pushed it toward Flynn, deciding not to beat around the bush. 'You once said to me that everyone here is running away from something, so what brought you here?'

Brown flecks flashed against green, his eyes defiant. 'I lived here for a couple of years as a child and I thought I'd come back.'

Surprise rocked through her. So that was why he seemed to belong so well. But she wasn't going to let him fox her with sidetracking. She studied his face, tight with tension. 'So you'd always planned to work up here?'

He met her gaze for a moment and then it slid away. 'Not exactly.' He took a long drink from the cold glass, his Adam's apple moving rhythmically against his strong neck.

She held onto coherent thought by a thread and took a sip of her drink.

His long fingers tracked across the circle of condensation on the table, the lines of moisture converging into a wide puddle. 'I'd survived a gruelling selection process and had accepted a position at Central Brisbane Hospital and was about to commence dermatology.'

Mineral water spurted into her nose and she immediately started to cough. She couldn't imagine Flynn working in one of the least exciting branches of medicine, and working regular hours inside a large hospital. 'Dermatology?'

He shot her an accusatory look. 'What?'

She wiped her mouth with a tissue. 'It's just that I can't picture you in that role. I'm not sure dermatology would really have suited you.'

He stared at her for a moment, his expression almost contemplative before it hardened. 'Yeah, well, it didn't work out. Turns out I was just the understudy in my own life when I thought I had the lead role.'

'Pardon?' She had no idea what he meant but her gut clenched at the antagonism in his voice.

His mouth firmed into a grim line and he spat out the words, precise and harsh. 'My fiancée—the one that was so keen for me to do family-friendly dermatology— stood me up at our wedding in front of three hundred friends and peers. She eloped with my best man.'

His pain speared her. No wonder he didn't want to go to the wedding. 'Oh, that totally sucks. And you had no idea?' She caught his searing look. 'I'm sorry, stupid question. Of course you wouldn't have.' She thought of Steven, who had bailed on her but in less public circumstances, and for the first time in a year was able to think slightly more kindly toward him.

He folded his arms across his chest. 'Even in hindsight I didn't have a clue.'

'We only see what we want to.' She wanted to take some of his pain away but her words sounded hollow.

His jaw tightened. 'Well, in that case, I guess I wanted to believe that neither Brooke, who professed to love me, nor my best mate, who was like a brother to me, would rip my heart out. I got that wrong.' He slammed his fist into the palm of his hand, making a slapping sound.

She touched his arm. 'Those are reasonable expectations, Flynn. Trust is part of love. Love can't happen without it.'

He picked up his drink and her arm fell away. 'Yeah, well, I'm not up for that much these days.'

Her heart ached for him and unexpected anger against his fiancée and friend simmered inside her. 'So Brooke and...'

'Dan.' He ran his hand through his hair. 'Yes, I believe they're still together living in *our* house.' He flicked her a look. 'We don't exchange Christmas cards.'

'They're living in *your* house!' Her indignation flooded over the words.

A bitter smile tugged at his lips. 'Oh, it's a good story. It's got all the elements—heart-warming friendship, money, lust and betrayal. It would make a good telemovie.'

His biting humour lanced her and she bit her lip. 'I'd offer you a drink but...'

This time his smile was wry and warm. 'Yeah, but the clinic's a dry zone.' He leaned back on his chair, a resigned look on his face. 'Dan and I had been mates since high school. We pretty much did everything together, even medicine. We shared digs at uni and then when we graduated and were sick of paying rent, we bought an old terrace house in inner Brisbane, complete with a rusting wrought-iron lace veranda. It was tumbling down around us.'

She caught a hint of a happy memory cross his face. 'The ultimate renovator's dream?'

'More like a nightmare, but some days it was very cathartic to come home from work and rip out a wall.' His jaw tightened. 'I met Brooke when she was a final-year medical student, not too long after we'd bought the house, and the three of us renovated it together.'

'Brooke and Dan didn't get along very well and they had some monumental clashes. But I desperately wanted my future wife and best friend to be good friends. Dan and I had been mates since boarding school and he'd been with me during some tough times with my family. I didn't want to be in the situation where I got married but lost my best friend.'

Mia tried to keep her face neutral but felt her brows draw in as the paradox struck her.

Flynn grimaced. 'I know, pretty ironic considering the outcome.'

She had crazy desire to defend him to himself. 'I think it was the aim of a caring and loving guy.'

His look of derision silenced her.

'Anyway, I became the peacemaker. I actively pushed them together so they could try and get to know each other. I did a hell of good job. Dan not only got the girl, he got the house.'

Outrage pounded her. 'But I don't understand how they ended up with the house.'

'When Brooke and I got engaged I thought the house would have to be sold but as the wedding got closer, Dan offered to sell his share to us so it could be our home. Brooke was so enthusiastic about the idea, saying how much she wanted to raise children in a house renovated by love, that I ended up agreeing.'

His abrupt laugh was full of scorn. 'Never fall in love, Mia. It makes a complete fool out you.'

She knew that all too well, but this was his story so she stayed silent.

Flynn's foot started to tap against the floor, his leg rigid with tension. 'Dan and I had power of attorney for each other. When the bank called about the transfer papers, I was caught up at the hospital in A and E in the middle of dealing with multiple burns victims after an apartment block had caught fire. The wedding was two days away and Dan offered to go with Brooke to the bank.'

Realisation thudded through her. 'They bought your share instead of selling his? But surely you could have contested that in court?'

'I could have.' His voice sounded flat in the quiet room. 'But the humiliation of standing at the altar with three hundred pairs of eyes staring at me and announcing that my wedding was off, combined with the whispers that followed me around at work for the next few months, was enough.'

She wanted to wrap her arms around him and stroke away the pain of his betrayal. 'And Kirra was a long way from Brisbane?'

'Got it in one.' He shifted in his seat. 'And that's my story.'

Except she had a niggling feeling that he hadn't told her everything. 'So how long are you planning on hiding here?'

He flicked her an intransigent look. 'I'm not hiding. I'm living and working.'

She pushed on. 'But you don't get to meet many women here.'

'That would be the plan.'

The growl in his voice told her to back off and, as much as she didn't want to, she decided she would, for now because she didn't want to alienate him. Meanwhile she was glad she wasn't in Brisbane because she had an irrational urge to let down Brooke and Dan's tyres, spraypaint their yuppie front fence and prank-call them at three in the morning.

She suddenly realized that today's church service would be the first time Flynn had been to a wedding since his own. No wonder he'd tried so hard to avoid it. An hour ago she'd pictured herself sitting in church with one of the school teachers but now she knew that wouldn't be possible.

She had to go to the wedding with Flynn.

Just thinking about sitting next to Flynn in a narrow and cramped pew, shoulders brushing, thighs touching, had her blood pounding with need. For her own peace of mind, going to the wedding with Flynn was the last thing she should be doing.

But she had little choice. They both had to go and clearly she couldn't let him go alone. She leaned forward. 'I totally understand how weddings aren't your thing.'

He raised his brows. 'So I'm off the hook for today?'

She took a steadying breath. 'No.'

'No.' The small word oozed resignation.

She put her hand over his, in a gesture of support. 'We're going to this wedding together. We'll go to the church service, congratulate the bride and groom, congratulate Susie and then leave. It's our job.'

He stared at her for a long time, his eyes filled with a jumble of emotions. His free hand came to rest over hers, his heat burning through her, racing deep down inside her, igniting longing and fuelling need.

Eventually he spoke. 'You're right. It's just part of the job.'

But suddenly the job had just got a lot more complicated.

'Well, the bride turned up. That has to be a good start to a happy married life.' Flynn pulled off his silk tie and unbuttoned the two top buttons of his shirt as relief rolled through him.

Mia shot him a penetrating look. 'I thought it all went off very well. The bride looked gorgeous, and Susie was so proud she almost burst. And you faced a personal challenge and got through it.' She suddenly giggled and relaxed back in the garden chair. 'You'll get so good at weddings you'll start crashing them.'

'I think those three sips of champagne you had addled your brain.'

He and Mia were sitting in her garden under a sprawling mahogany tree strung with tiny bud lights, their twinkling white glow a precursor to the stars that were slowly rising in the night sky. Most of the wedding guests had gone on to the reception but, as Mia had promised him, they had left as soon as they had walked down the official bridal party line and wished everyone well. From the moment they had driven to the church right up to the time they'd returned to her house, Mia hadn't left his side.

And when the priest had announced the arrival of the bride she'd reached for his hand and held it until the happy couple had left the church. It had been the act of a true friend. Except the wondrous feelings her touch had stirred up in him didn't belong in the same sentence as friendship.

He breathed out a long breath. 'I think I'll leave the wedding crashing to you.'

'They're not really my scene either.' She slipped off her strappy sandals and wriggled her toes, her red nail polish shining like a channel beacon.

He watched, mesmerised as the ripple of movement trailed up her foot, along the curves of her calves, and over her knees before disappearing under the shimmery sea-green fabric of her dress. He pulled his mind back from the imagined image of her thighs. 'Not your scene? Most women love a wedding and the idea of a happy-ever-after.'

Her relaxed demeanour stiffened slightly. 'I'm not most women, and happy-ever-afters are overrated.'

A red flag shot up in his brain and he studied her face carefully. The sadness in her eyes, which he'd attributed to the loss of her family, had receded a small amount over the last couple of weeks, but now it was back and firmly entrenched. Her comment snagged and he couldn't let it go. After all, the death of her mother and brother shouldn't affect her opinion on marriage.

He tried a flippant approach in the hope he could sneak under her defences and get her to open up. 'Don't tell me you were stood up at the altar, too.'

She shook her head slowly. 'Not quite. You get to keep the gold medal for that event.'

A tiny smile tugged at her lips, almost distracting him. 'But you were engaged?'

She looked up at him through long, thick lashes. 'I was for a few months, but Steven couldn't cope with…' She paused and took in a deep breath. 'Steven decided he didn't want to marry into my family.'

He immediately thought of his mother. 'I'm sorry. I know how family politics and money can nuke relationships.'

She shrugged. 'As it turned out, it was for the best.'

'I gather all this happened before your mother and brother died?' He was trying to piece it all together.

She clasped her hands in her lap and nodded. 'Actually, it happened soon after my brother's death.' She jutted her chin forward defiantly. 'As they say, timing is everything.'

Her hurt pounded him and he wanted to thump the man who had compounded her grief. But at the same time confusion swirled in his brain. 'Your brother's death? I assumed your mother and brother died together in an accident?'

Silently, she picked up a box of matches from the small table and rose to her feet.

He kept his gaze fixed on her as she padded over to

the citronella flares. With studied concentration she struck a match and the hiss of sulphur igniting was the only sound between them. Flames leapt into the air, the smoke, which would follow, designed to drive back the mosquitoes.

Her silence told him more than her previous words. She didn't want to talk about this but with a patience he'd learned on Kirra he waited for her to find her time to speak.

She turned, tumbling the matchbox over and over between her fingers. 'Michael's car ran off the road into a tree a few months before my mother died.'

The sequence of events seemed muddled in his mind. Getting information from Mia was like getting blood from a stone, but a growing need to know more about her drove him on. He stood up and walked over to her. 'So your mother died from injuries sustained in the accident?'

Hesitation wafted through her eyes and she sighed. 'No. My mother wasn't involved in the accident, although losing Michael probably didn't help her health. She'd been unwell and failing for a long time.'

Still the information dribbled out in a frustrating and ambiguous way. The doctor in him needed to know, the man wanted to understand. 'Cancer?'

She raised her gaze to his, grief vivid and raw in her blue eyes. He saw the battle of emotions raging, as if she didn't want to tell him. He caught the moment she capitulated.

'My mother died of dementia.'

The modern scourge of an aging population. A condition that touched so many families. He immediately knew that she would have put her life on hold to care for her elderly mother. She would have had to endure the powerlessness of watching a loved one fade away. 'You really have had a horrendously tough year.'

Instinctively, he reached out and trailed his fingers down her smooth cheek. 'I wish I could do something to make it better.'

She raised her hand, and for a moment her palm covered his as her gaze stared into him, terrifyingly empty and bereft.

And then it flared with unconcealed desire.

She wanted him as much as he wanted her.

Weeks of restraint dropped away and he reached for her, curving his hands around her cheeks, glorying in the weight of her body against his own and longing to feel her lips under his.

She pressed soft and pliant lips to the corner of his mouth. Lips that brushed his with a touch so gentle and yet so potent that his blood pounded through him hard and fast, and the boom of an explosion rocked him.

Mia gave a cry of surprise and jumped back from him as if she'd taken a volt of electricity. Her hand flew to her chest and then she laughed as her gaze tilted upwards. 'Look, fireworks.' She excitedly pointed to the sky as pink and blue lights trailed through the sky.

The explosions he'd heard had been real. His head spun from a lack of blood, all of which had pooled in groin. He felt like a sixteen-year-old boy disabled by lust. Dragging in a deep breath, he tried to find his equilibrium as the squeal of a rocket screamed around them. 'Someone must have brought them back from Darwin and saved them from the Territory celebrations. Let's hope they've read the instructions.'

'I love fireworks.' She smiled at him, the colours of the magnesium dust reflected in her eyes. 'They make you forget everything for a moment and give you joy.'

He knew another way they could both drive away the demons of their past and find joy. He watched her with her head tilted up to the sky, her face free of the grief that usually shadowed her.

He wanted to feel her body curving against his, breathe in the lemon scent of her hair, the intoxicating richness of her perfume, and taste her sweetness. He hadn't wanted a woman in two years but tonight he wanted to lose himself in her. He raised his arm in preparation to slide it around her waist and draw her back close to him. To kiss her until they both melted to the ground in a pool of need.

The shrillness of the clinic's emergency siren broke over them.

Adrenaline crashed into disappointment with a sickening thud. Obviously tonight wasn't going to work but the seed for seduction had been sown. He just had to get the timing right.

Mia ran barefoot to the clinic, the emergency thankfully dousing the simmering lust that had consumed her moments before. She'd lost all sense tonight. She'd half kissed Flynn and that was such a bad idea for so many reasons.

And what had possessed her to mention her mother's dementia? She hadn't meant to but the look of empathy in Flynn's eyes when she'd talked about Steven had lowered her guard. Most people associated Alzheimer's with dementia and never thought of the insidious Pick's disease, so her secret was probably still safe. 'Do you think Alice has deteriorated?'

'No.' The moonlight showed his grim expression. 'I'd say someone's come to grief with a cracker.'

They ran up into the clinic and met a chaotic scene. People were yelling and wailing as they crowded in on the door.

'Stand back, now!'

She'd never heard Flynn's voice sound so stern but it did the job. The crowd opened up and she and Flynn raced into the treatment room.

A young man writhing in pain lay on the examination table, his face swollen and blistered, pale pink against his normally black skin.

Jenny stood helplessly wringing her hands. 'The crackers blew up in his face.'

'Get the crash cart.'

But as Flynn's curt words sounded, Mia had already pulled it into position. Using shears, she cut away the half-burned T-shirt, exposing more burns on the man's chest. She looked at Jenny. 'What's his name?'

'Jai.'

'Jai, we're going to help you.' She bit her lip and glanced at Flynn. 'I'll ring Darwin.'

Flynn shook his head. 'No, I need you here. He needs two IV lines, his eyes need a saline lavage and we'll probably have to intubate.' He pulled his stethoscope up to his ears. 'Jenny, get wet packs for Jai's face and chest.

We need to cool his skin. After you've done that, get Darwin on the phone and tell them we have severe facial burns and to send the air ambulance. I'll talk to them as soon as Jai's stable.'

'Yes, Doctor.' Jenny headed toward the cupboard with the sterile packs.

Mia hesitated, wondering where to put the monitor dots. 'His chest is burned and the monitor dots—'

'It can't be helped.' Flynn was in triage mode. 'Put the dots onto the burned skin. We need levels.'

She ripped the backing paper off and quickly put the dots in place, trying not to think about how the burned skin would eventually come off with the dot. A moment later the ECG bleeped reassuringly but she knew that hypovolaemic shock and a constricted airway were their biggest challenges.

Flynn pulled the stethoscope out of his ears. 'He's developing stridor.'

She pulled open a drawer on the cart. 'Do you want to intubate first or put in the IV lines?' Both were vital.

'We'll keep a close eye on him and put the lines in first. That way, if he arrests we'll have access for drugs.'

'He needs morphine as soon as possible.' She passed Flynn a tourniquet, alcohol swab and cannula. 'You start and I'll have the line primed by the time you're in.'

'Thanks.' A smile carved through the worry that lined his face, travelling along his cheeks, unusually free of stubble.

She soaked up his smile, letting it trail through her, lighting her up from the inside and warming her in a way she'd never known before.

It's just a smile of thanks. It's not specifically for you.
But she ignored the voice and held onto the feeling.

Clamping the IV tubing with her hand, she let the Hartmann's solution fill the chamber before letting go and releasing the liquid in one quick gush to avoid air bubbles.

She hung the litre bag of fluid onto the pole.

'I'm in.' Flynn withdrew the trocar and connected the drip. 'You insert one into his left arm and I'll check his breathing.'

Mia wrapped the blood-pressure cuff around Jai's arm and pumped it up. 'BP one hundred on sixty.' She re-pumped the cuff, using the band of pressure to make the young man's veins rise. 'Jai, just one more needle and then we'll give you something for the pain.'

Jai's only response was a moan through lips swollen to three times their normal size.

Mia's heart tore. He must be in agony. Her fingers palpated the largest vein and she slid the needle in quickly, surprised Jai wasn't more peripherally shut down. Grabbing an ampoule, she snapped it open and with a skill honed over many years she drew up the clear liquid into the syringe. 'Check ten milligrams of morphine.'

Flynn read the ampoule. 'Check. When you're ready, please set up for a tracheostomy.'

She plunged the morphine into the rubber bung of the IV. 'Do you think he has oesophageal and laryngeal burns?'

His black brows drew together. 'With all this swelling I can't imagine I'd be able to visualise the vocal cords, let alone pass an endotracheal tube.' He walked to the sink and washed his hands.

Mia quickly assembled what they needed—a scalpel, Betadine, tracheostomy tube, suture thread, saline and a syringe to fill the balloon of the tube. Opening a sterile cloth, she draped it over a trolley and then added two pairs of gloves, along with the other items.

'Jai, I have to tilt your head back.' With both hands gloved, she carefully placed them against his ears and hyper-extended their patient's neck. Then she picked up his hand. 'You'll feel the sting of the local anaesthetic and after that just some pushing and pulling.'

Jai murmured something incomprehensible and she hoped the morphine had sedated him.

Flynn snapped on his gloves and infiltrated the area with local anaesthetic before swabbing it. 'Just in case you ever have to do this, the trachea is generally two finger-breadths above the sternal notch.' He demonstrated how to measure.

She concentrated on his every word and action. He always did this—he turned every situation into a teaching one and generously passed on his knowledge. The more time she spent with him, the more she realised what a special man he truly was. Did Brooke have any idea what she'd given up?

A bubble of anger burst inside her at the pain that woman had caused him, was still causing him, and she found herself vigorously snapping the scalpel onto the blade handle and slapping it into his palm. 'So it's a horizontal cut.'

'Yes, it is. Right through the skin and muscle, and down to the third or fourth ring of cartilage.' He dextrously cut and enlarged, ready for the tube. 'Pass the tube.'

With one hand she swabbed the blood that oozed from the cut and with the other she picked up the tube. 'How much pressure do you need to apply to insert the tube?'

He frowned as he tried to insert the plastic tube. 'More than you think you need.'

She gave him a dry smile. 'That's about as precise as my grandmother saying, "Add a glug of soda water" to a recipe.'

The deep grooves that bracketed his mouth twitched. 'Medicine isn't always precise but the moment you feel the resistance disappear you know that the tube is in the trachea.' He leaned toward Jai. 'Just breathe normally, Jai.' He immediately checked Jai's respirations using his stethoscope.

Mia could see the rise and fall of Jai's chest and his respirations were less rapid. 'You're in the right place?'

'I am.' Dimples carved deeply into his cheeks, giving him a look that radiated waves of charisma.

Charisma that showered down on her, releasing a jet of desire, which blasted its way through her. The room swayed. She quickly injected saline into the balloon of the tube to hold it in place, glad she had a reason to lower her gaze because without one it would have been stuck like glue to Flynn's face.

'Now we've maintained his airway, I want you to clean Jai's eyes and I'll stitch this in place.'

Flynn's voice was all business, as it should be. She was the one being unprofessional with these crazy flushes of desire. She gave herself a shake and briskly twisted the top off the saline.

She only had room-temperature saline, which should

be warm enough but would probably feel cold to Jai. 'I have to clean your face now and it might feel cold.' The magnesium dust from the cracker had impregnated his eyes and skin.

Being as gentle as she could, she poured the saline over his eyes and wiped from the inner aspect outwards, removing as much muck as she could. Blindness was a real possibility.

The young man shuddered under her ministrations and she hated causing him more discomfort. He had a long road ahead of him. 'Normally I'd put cling wrap on burns but these are filthy. What do you want me to use?'

'Wash them with chlorhexidine and then slather them with SSD cream.' Flynn snipped the suture thread with the scissors. 'Jenny, what time is the air ambulance expected?'

'It left Darwin. Should be here at nine. They sending a doctor and nurse. Walter, he gone to light fires at the airstrip.' Jenny turned to go. 'I go see Alice.'

'Thanks, Jenny.' Mia smiled at the worried health worker as she disappeared out the door. She turned back to Flynn. 'If they're an hour away, should we catheterise him so we have an accurate fluid picture?'

Flynn nodded. 'Good idea. I'll do that, you clean up the burns.'

They worked together, anticipating each other, falling into an unspoken routine driven by the emergency mantra. They'd established an airway, maintained circulating volume, and were now dealing with the burns.

She kept sneaking glances at Flynn as he worked, watching how his hair curled over his collar, how his hair had a few silver strands at his temples, and how gentle his hands were with Jai.

For weeks she'd been telling herself he was just a doctor. Her occasional doctor. Sure, she'd been attracted to him but she'd been able to put that aside. But today she'd learned too much about him for her to think of him only as a sexy doctor. When he'd told her his story, he'd moved from colleague to wounded man. A man who needed a friend. It had seemed as natural as breathing to hold his hand in the church and give him the support she knew she would have welcomed had she been in the same situation.

And tonight he'd returned her friendship with his caring concern for her and she'd misconstrued it for something else. In a moment of insanity she'd tried to kiss him with a pathetic brush of lips that had been more on his cheek than his mouth. Thank goodness for the fireworks which had arrived with perfect timing, saving her from further embarrassment.

Flynn was hiding out on Kirra and wanted no part of a relationship.

Not that she could offer him that even if he wanted one.

A sudden thought, clear and dazzling, burst in her head. Perhaps they'd met so she could help him move on, show him that the actions of one woman shouldn't derail his life. Perhaps her job was to bring him back from hiding and make him realise how much he was missing by retreating from the world.

Flynn deserved the happy-ever-after she'd never know, and she was determined he would have it.

CHAPTER SEVEN

MIA placed the phone back on its cradle.

'How is he?' Jenny asked the same question she'd asked every morning. It had been a week since Jai had been airlifted to Darwin and soon after transferred south to Adelaide for specialist burns treatment.

'He's still in Intensive Care but they're weaning him off the respirator so this is good news.' Mia tried to sound positive but it was early days yet. Burns victims often faced their hardest challenge a couple of weeks after the initial injury.

'He's not coming home for a long time.' Susie sighed and patted Jenny's shoulder.

Mia nodded as Susie spoke the words she hadn't wanted to say. When islanders left Kirra they often pined for their beloved home, their well-being so intrinsically linked to their traditional lands. Not only did Jai have a huge physical battle on his hands, he was also a thousand kilometres from his home and his family.

'But as soon as he's well enough he'll be transferred back to Darwin and then his family can visit him and we can organise a roster of people to go over.' Mia scribbled an idea on a yellow sticky note. 'Perhaps we can raise some money for ferry fares by having a fete?'

Susie's white teeth flashed as she smiled. 'That's a good idea, Sis.'

Happiness spread through Mia. She constantly trod a fine line, being the non-indigenous team member. She was there to teach, not to preach, and not every idea she had worked but this one seemed to be well received. 'We could ask the child-care centre to do face painting and have a barbecue stall and…' She caught sight of Flynn who had unexpectedly appeared in the doorway, as was his wont. 'And we could have a dunk tank with Dr Flynn as the target.'

'Hey, I heard that!' Flynn sounded affronted but his hazel eyes crinkled in a warm smile, which he directed straight at her.

She hugged it close.

The two health workers giggled.

'That Jimmy, he has a good throwing arm,' Susie teased, before turning to Mia. 'All nurses get taken on bush camp and your turn is tomorrow.'

'Bush camp? What's that?'

'We take you out and tell you about bush tucker and bush medicine. We all camp out and you cook dinner for us.' Susie spoke as if this was an everyday event.

'Really?' She glanced at Flynn for confirmation. He'd walked over to her whiteboard, which actually looked yellow due to the number of sticky notes stuck to it.

He turned back from reading the board and gave her a knowing smile. 'Really.'

A strand of unease started to vibrate inside her, and

she had an overwhelming feeling she was on the outside of an 'in' joke. 'Hang on a minute, let me get this straight. During the day, you collect the food for me to cook that night?'

'No, you have to gather or catch food first.' Susie grinned cheekily. 'But I can light the fire for you.'

Visions of being very hungry stamped themselves all over her brain. 'Do I have to build my own bark humpy as well?'

Jenny giggled. 'No, we use tents.'

The two health workers ambled off to give their community the latest news of Jai.

She slapped the sticky note about the fete onto her whiteboard and turned to see Flynn studying her, his expression uncharacteristically serious. 'What do you know about this?'

'It's something they do when they like you.'

She chuckled with scepticism. 'What, take me out into the bush and leave me to starve?'

His sober look vanished with a wink. 'You'll only starve if you're lousy at fishing or a bad spear thrower.'

Laughter bubbled up, bringing with it a sensation of pure joy. 'Thank you so much. That information is very reassuring.'

'It's a great opportunity to experience some Kirri culture.'

She knew it would be. 'I'm really honoured I've been asked even if I am going to be hungry.' She sat down on the edge of the desk, catching the scent of his aftershave and enjoying the freshness of the citrus tang. 'I kind of like the idea of a women-only camp, sitting around the fire talking about some of the common issues that are faced by women around the world.'

He leaned back, his fingers lacing behind his head, and his hair shone like jet in the stream of sunshine coming through the window. As he stretched, tensed biceps pushed against the soft cotton of his shirt, which rode up, exposing a band of washboard, flat stomach.

Mia gulped in a breath at the sight of toned muscles and sun-tanned skin. Skin that made her fingers tingle and long to touch it.

She quickly grasped her previous and safer train of thought. 'You know, issues like domestic violence, dealing with a partner with an addiction and parenting issues. Shared stuff like that crosses cultural boundaries and...' Her voice trailed away as she caught a wicked yet intoxicating glint in his eyes. 'What?'

His laugh rumbled around her—warm and delicious like hot, chocolate sauce.

'I hate to disappoint you but I'm coming, too.'

A surge of emotion whipped her but no way could she call it disappointment. 'Oh, so basically this is a "roast Mia" situation?' She gave a wry smile. 'I'm glad I'll be providing so much entertainment for so many.'

'You're good value that way.' But the words came out on a smile. 'In fact, seeing as it's a long weekend and there are no visiting specialists tomorrow, I thought we could head out in an hour or so and get a twenty-four-hour head start. I could give you a few tips so you actually have a chance of finding some food when we meet up with the others tomorrow.'

Flynn and her camping out together. *Alone.* Her

breath caught in her throat. *Stop it. He's just being his normal self and back in teacher mode again.* 'You'd help me cheat?'

He grinned. 'It's not cheating, just a bit of advanced information. Besides, it will be fun to see the looks on their faces when you actually present them with a feast.'

'A feast?' She shook her head in disbelief. 'You have the skills to help me do that?'

His smile raced through the stubble around his lips, streaked along his cheeks and into his eyes. Eyes filled with the thrill of a challenge. 'Mia, I have skills and talents you've yet to discover.'

And, so help her, she wanted to discover them.

Mia couldn't remember enjoying herself so much as she had in the last few hours. Flynn had taken the meaning of 'off road' to new heights, negotiating the four-wheel-drive vehicle around palms and ancient cycads, bouncing it over rocks, and driving it across scorched and blackened earth.

So far she'd eaten green ants, which had an aroma of very strong English mustard but tasted like lemon and were loaded with vitamin C. She'd dipped her finger in 'sugarbag', the honey of the native bees, and been told that she could eat all of the waterlily and the stem made a good straw.

Her head was buzzing with information. 'How can you tell where you are? It all looks pretty much the same to me.'

He gave her an indulgent smile. 'I used to come out this way a lot when I was a kid. There are some lovely waterholes in the area and it was one of the few places Mum enjoyed.'

She pricked up her ears. Flynn had never mentioned his family much. 'How long did you live here?'

'Two years. I was eleven when we arrived.' He turned the vehicle onto a dirt track. 'My parents managed the art centre and helped the Kirri find distribution outlets for their art. Mum managed the small island gallery and Dad was mostly involved in the carving side of things.' His face relaxed as if good memories were coming back to him. 'It was dad who recognised Walter's talent and encouraged him to start carving as a career.'

It was one of the few places Mum enjoyed. 'But your mum didn't enjoy living here?'

Immediately the muscles in his neck tightened. 'Mum loved it here for the first six months but, just like the two previous places we'd lived, after the newness wore off she wanted to leave. That's why each weekend I would ask to come out to this part of the island because when she was here she was happier. We'd sit on the top of the bright red cliffs and watch the dugong play, and I'd ask her not to leave.'

Her heart tore for the young Flynn. 'And it worked? She stuck it out for two years?' Mia held onto the handle over the door to steady herself as the truck hit a huge pothole.

Flynn crashed through the gears with more force than necessary. 'She left the day after my thirteenth birthday. She took me south to Brisbane, dropped me off at boarding school, arranged to meet me in two weeks then kissed me goodbye and left me.'

Left me. 'Until the arranged meeting?'

'No.' His expression hardened. 'I waited three hours for her in a shopping mall, as planned. She never showed. When I rang Dad he had no idea she'd left him, he thought she was on two weeks' holidays but, in fact, she'd left us both.' He swung the wheel hard right, just missing a wallaby that had jumped out in front of them. 'We didn't hear a thing for six months and then she sent me a letter saying she was living in San Francisco with an American artist she'd met in Melbourne.'

Her stomach rolled at the emotional pain he must have experienced as he wondered why his mother had vanished. 'So you visited in the holidays?' Mia asked the question against the anxiety that a woman who would disappear for six months wasn't one hundred per cent emotionally well.

He flung her a look of incredulity. 'Oh, did I forget to mention the part where she said she needed to divest herself of her past, so she could finally find the happiness that had eluded her all her life?'

She stifled a gasp. She couldn't imagine a mother ever inferring that their child wasn't one of the greatest joys of their life. And do it to a thirteen-year-old who would be battling his own hormonal demons. 'She must have been depressed.'

He pulled the truck to a stop under a large pandanus palm. 'Perhaps. At thirteen I didn't have the clinical skills to make an accurate diagnosis.' The sharp tone in his voice revealed his hurt. 'At thirty I had the skills and I know Brooke wasn't depressed. She left of her own free will, just like my mother, with no note and no warning. There's something about the Harrington men that makes women leave.'

She couldn't believe he'd said that. 'That's utter nonsense.' Her words rushed out fervently. 'You had a go at me about fate and yet here you are taking two un-related incidents and trying to connect them. A woman who loves you stays with you. Brooke didn't love you.'

Hazel eyes sparked with antagonism. 'And my mother?'

His words hit her hard and fast like a cricket ball in a head-high full toss. She didn't have an easy answer to his question but viscerally she knew that his interpreta-tion was very wrong.

She opened her mouth to speak but Flynn had opened his door and was moving out of the truck, running as if he was competing in the one hundred-metre sprint.

Had he left to stop the conversation? She wasn't certain but then she saw a flash of movement and realised he was chasing something. She grabbed her camera and started to jog after him, giving thanks for the fifth time that day that she was wearing sturdy hiking boots, as this was snake country.

He suddenly stopped, his hands on his thighs, his chest heaving. He caught his breath and grinned at her. 'Bandicoot. Man, they can move fast.'

'I couldn't even see it! Surely there are slower-moving things for dinner.' She glanced around, still feeling like an alien on another planet.

He straightened up, running the back of his hand across his brow. 'You have to tune into your senses, Mia.

I think you've forgotten how to do that. Sticky notes don't work out here.'

She caught a fleeting look of disapproval but let the comment pass. 'So eyes, ears and nose.'

He nodded. 'That's right. Let's look around here for starters.' He pointed to his left. 'See that gumtree with the bright orange flowers? Those flowers mean that it's time to start burning the land. When they burn it sends the wildlife scurrying so that's good hunting. Then six weeks later, when the new shoots start, the wildlife comes back to feed on the succulents.'

She started to follow his line of thinking. 'And there's no protective vegetation so they're easy to spot so easier to hunt.'

His eyes flashed approvingly. 'Excellent deduction, Ms Latham.' He draped his arm casually around her shoulder. 'See, you really don't need to write everything down. You have an incisive mind, you just need to trust it.'

She looked into eyes filled with support and good intentions and her heart turned over.

Trust won't help stop a genetically predetermined deterioration. She pushed the thought aside. Today she refused to think about her future or more realistically her lack of a future. And she wasn't thinking about the past either. Today she was living for the moment out in the Kirra bush with the most fascinating man she'd ever met. 'What's that spindly-looking sapling with the lone yellow flower?'

'Kapok.'

'Really, as in the white fluffy stuff that used to be in pillows?'

'That's right. This tree tells a big story, too. When the kapok flowers it means the crocodiles and turtles are laying their eggs, and the kangaroos are plump and healthy and make good tucker.'

Mia shuddered at the thought of crocodiles. 'As I couldn't ever throw a javelin, I doubt kangaroo will be on the menu.'

Flynn laughed. 'On Kirra hunting is still a really important part of community life but they're not averse to using a rifle when it suits them.'

His arm still lingered on her shoulder as he turned and gently steered her toward the truck. 'But if we're going to be traditional, as the man I do the hunting and you do the gathering.'

She raised her brows. 'Is that so?'

The flirting glint was back. 'Absolutely, and I've got a special place in mind.'

She stopped and in mock indignation she folded her arms across her chest, enjoying their banter. 'Had I known I would have brought my bark basket with me.'

'Not to worry. I have a plastic bucket in the back of the truck.' He quickly ran and grabbed the vivid yellow bucket.

She shook her head in amazement at the lurid colour. 'Obviously we don't need to be camouflaged. I bet you could probably see that bucket on a satellite picture.'

Dimples appeared in his cheeks. 'Crocodiles like a bright colour.'

Fear gushed through her, draining the blood from her face. Snakes she could handle but the thought of the prehistoric creatures that could move with such deathly speed terrified her.

'Hey.' His fingers suddenly brushed her chin, tilting it upward. He spoke softly. 'I'm joking. I'd never put you into danger.'

She gazed into eyes dark with remorse, dusky with care and light with something else she couldn't quite pin down.

He had so much care to give. He deserved to find a woman who would stay with him and love him.

Caught in his penetrating gaze it was almost all she could do to nod her understanding but she somehow managed to find her voice. 'Sorry. I know you wouldn't put us in peril—it's just that I have this thing about crocodiles.'

'Most of us do.' He dropped his fingers from her chin, caught her hand in his and together they started walking.

'Kirra has salt-water crocodiles in the ocean and strolls along the water's edge are out. But there are no crocodiles in this area and when I got permission from the traditional owners to bring you out here, I checked again.'

'Thanks.'

'You're most welcome.'

His smile sent quivering trails of delight through her and she squeezed his hand in appreciation, loving the feel of his palm against hers.

The bush got thicker and he dropped her hand, needing both arms to bush-bash and hold up branches so she could duck under them. She followed behind, admiring his athleticism and the way his shorts moved across what she imagined was a taut behind.

'Ooh-h.' Her foot suddenly sank up to her ankles into blue-grey mud and she swung her head around, taking in her environs. She'd been so busy being gloriously distracted by Flynn that she hadn't noticed the change in vegetation. Low spindly trees with bright green leaves and exposed roots surrounded her.

'Mangroves.' She lifted her foot up with a sucking squelch and tried to stand on a large root. 'We're gathering food in mangroves?' She couldn't hide her disbelief.

His eyes twinkled. 'Nature's nursery. Come on, there's some fabulous food here.' He strode off, oblivious to the mud, a man on a mission.

She gingerly took another step, which sent mud flicking onto her calves before her feet immediately disappeared into more mud. She stepped carefully again but still mud splattered her legs.

It's only mud. Live for the moment—you don't know how long you've got.

Flynn, now twenty metres ahead, turned and gave her a wave and a smile. A smile with a magnetic force field that encircled her, pulling her toward him.

She plunged her feet into the mud and waded, closing the distance between them.

He squatted down. 'This is what you're looking for as you walk.' He ran his finger along criss-crossing trails in the mud before digging down under the roots of the mangrove. A moment later he triumphantly held aloft a large black shell.

'What is it?' She peered at the long spiral shell.

'A whelk. It's a sea snail. We cook them in the coals and they taste brilliant.' He tossed it into the bucket and then quickly harvested a dozen.

'Now it's your turn.'

She stared at the mud, trying not to think about what

could be hidden in it, and plunged her hand into the soggy depths. As the mud squished between her fingers she couldn't help herself and a girly squeal escaped from her lips. She quickly pulled her hand back, the sudden action making her overbalance, and sat down hard in the mud.

Flynn's mirth rang out loud and clear.

Resignation and amusement spun through her as the water seeped through her cargo pants. 'You're really enjoying this, aren't you?'

His body shook with laughter. 'Probably more than I should.' He pulled his digital camera out of his pocket. 'Smile.'

She tilted her head, gave a pout and with a muddy hand flicked back her hair as if she were a model on a shoot.

The camera trembled in Flynn's hands before he steadied it and she heard the electronic sound of the shutter.

The moment he slid the camera back into his pocket she hurled a handful of mud at him, catching him on the shoulder.

'Hey!' For a second his face wore a stunned expression and then he grinned.

A grin of fun, a grin of pleasure. A grin of pure intent.

At that precise moment she realised she hadn't thought this through and she was a sitting duck for a retaliatory attack.

As his hand scooped up a large glop of mud, she hauled herself up, with one hand on a mangrove and the other filled with sludgy ammunition.

A chuckle wafted on the hot air and then mud caught her between the shoulder blades, the water dribbling down her back, cool in the midday heat. She threw wildly as she tried to gain her balance.

'You missed by a mile. I'm over here.'

Foolishly she turned, the action leaving her wide open and completely unprotected.

Mud splattered her neck and chest, sticking her T-shirt to her skin. 'You've done it now. I'm showing no mercy.' She flung her arm back and arced it forward, black goop flying through the air and hitting his arm.

'Right! That's it. When I catch you, you're going to be dunked in mud.'

Joy and delight surged through her as she ducked and darted through the mangroves, hurling mud and laughing more than she could ever remember.

Flynn had the aim of a marksman and rarely missed. She, on the other hand, was being outplayed and outmanoeuvred.

She recognised the ribbon Flynn had tied on the tree when they'd first arrived in the mangroves and she took a sharp left, seeking retreat, running back to firmer ground and away from the mud.

She heard the crack and snap of vegetation and knew Flynn had followed her. Panting with exertion and doubled up with laughter, she held up her hands in surrender when he appeared in the clearing by the truck. 'I give up. You're too good.'

Dimples shone like stars in his cheeks. 'I am, aren't I?' He stood in front of her, tall, dark and deliciously mud splattered, holding the ridiculously bright yellow bucket. His eyes danced with devilment. 'Just remember that next time you start a mud fight with the master.'

Laughing, she shook her head at him before giving a mock bow. 'So, wise one, is there anywhere I can wash this stinking mud off me?' She pulled at her wet and filthy clothes.

His eyes darkened and his gaze seemed fixed on her shirt. 'I know the perfect place.' He swung the bucket into the back of the truck. 'Hop in.'

Mia pulled a couple of old towels out of her bag and spread them out to protect the seats, before unlacing her boots and pulling her feet from their soggy confines.

Flynn turned the key and the truck lurched forward over the rough ground. 'You'll love this place.' He turned and winked. 'There's no mud.'

'I'm liking it already.' She leaned back and as she lifted a drink bottle to her lips she gave in to an over-whelming need and sneaked sideways glances at Flynn. How could one man make her feel so alive in a way she'd never known before?

She dragged her gaze away and looked out the window. 'The vegetation's just got thicker.'

Flynn nodded approvingly, like a teacher with a student who was finally making progress. 'See, you're learning already. The thicker vegetation means water is close by.'

He stopped the vehicle and opened the door. 'It's only a short walk through that grove of paperbarks.'

Mia picked up the towels and clambered out of the vehicle, her wet pants sticking to her. Jamming her hat on her head, she didn't care what she looked like, she just wanted to immerse herself in cool, fresh water.

Flynn rounded the back of the truck, holding his battered hat in his left hand. His gaze lazily flicked from her head to her toes, spending time on the journey down.

Heat unfurled from deep within her, rolling out in waves.

He grabbed her hand. 'Prepare yourself for a treat.'

Is it you? The errant thought took hold as he led the way though the eucalypts.

She caught the glint of sunlight on water through the clumps of palms and lush vegetation and suddenly she was standing on the edge of a waterhole, fed by a rushing stream of fresh, sparkling water so clear that she could see tiny fish. Delicate ferns grew out of the mossy banks, the vivid green in stark contrast to the burnt brown and orange that characterised the land a mere two hundred metres away.

'Apart from the palms, I could be back in Tassie. I love it.'

Flynn beamed. 'I knew you would.' He dropped her hand and reached up, untangling a large rope, which hung from a sturdy gumtree. He pulled it forward, his grip firm, the muscles in his arms taut with definition. With an almighty yell he jumped out over the water and cannonballed into its depths.

Mia threw her head back in laughter as water sprayed all over her and mud ran in rivulets down her legs.

He reappeared a few seconds later, flicking water from his hair, his T-shirt hiding nothing as it moulded itself to his broad chest. 'It's magnificent.'

You're magnificent. She leaned over and caught the rope. 'Look out, I'm coming in.' She wrapped her hands round the coarse, damp rope and swung herself out over the water.

A feeling of freedom rushed through her as she sailed through the air, and when she let go of the rope she screamed, not from fear but because she could. Her toes hit the water, the chill racing up her legs, and then she was submerged in a blaze of refreshing bubbles.

She kicked up and swam until she could feel sand under her toes. She opened her eyes to find Flynn's hazel gaze seeking hers. 'This is glorious.'

He smiled a long, slow smile that sent mini-shock waves of pleasure rocking through her. His hand reached out and with the pad of his thumb he brushed away the remnants of the mud on her cheek. 'You're glorious. Even covered in mud you're completely sensational.' The words came out low and tremulous.

Her breath stalled in her throat as his fingers trailed along her jaw—a feather-light touch with incendiary properties. Her knees buckled and she gripped his arm.

His hand slowly curved behind her neck, and she moved toward him, drawn by the invisible force of attraction that had been building between them from the moment they'd met.

It was as if every bone in her body had dissolved and she could no longer support herself. She laid her head on his shoulder, with her chest pressed against his, feeling his heart pounding under her breast, and she knew at that moment this was exactly where she wanted to be.

She wanted *him*.

She was tired of fighting this overwhelming attraction. She wanted his arms wrapped tightly around her, his stubble grazing her cheek and his hot mouth working its magic all over her, leaving no place untouched. She wanted it all.

Live for the moment.

For the first time in her life she was going to take what she wanted and not worry about the future.

CHAPTER EIGHT

FLYNN gloried in the feel of Mia's wet body pressed against his own as his heart pounded his urgent need for her to every cell of his body. His lips trailed kisses along the curve of her ear and somehow he managed to speak through a hoarse throat. 'This thing between us, this simmering attraction, you feel it too, don't you?'

She slowly raised her head, unmistakable desire clear and bold in her sea-blue eyes. 'Oh, yes.'

His body tightened at her low and husky response. It took every ounce of his self-control not to plunder her mouth right there and then. She wanted him as much as he wanted her. 'Do you have a plan?'

A flash of something sparked for a second behind the desire in her eyes and then faded as fast as it had appeared. 'I don't make plans. I just take things day by day.' She raised her hand to his cheek. 'Right now I want to make love to you. It's as simple as that.'

Perfect. Her words released his corralled lust, the stampede of need stripping away almost all rational thought, but one small voice spoke up. *Women never see sex as simple.* He opened his mouth to reply but she immediately rested her forefinger against his lips, perception shining in her eyes and understanding lining her smile.

'Shh, don't panic. I don't expect you to marry me, I don't expect or want anything from you except this.' Her mouth tilted against his, her lips hot, hard and demanding.

White lights showered in his head, and with a moan he greedily returned the kiss, taking what she offered and seeking even more.

Wet arms snaked around his neck, fingers gripped his hair and her taste exploded in his mouth as wild as the honey they'd supped on earlier. He'd never experienced a kiss like it. Frank and unabashed lust danced with a poignant tenderness. With each and every wondrous exploration her mouth managed to give and take simultaneously, threatening to shatter the wall he'd so carefully constructed around his heart.

Mia suddenly found the thin barrier of wet clothing between them more than she could bear. She wanted to feel Flynn's skin against hers but she couldn't bear for her lips to abandon his so she tried to push his T-shirt up his back. But the wet fabric stuck like a second skin.

Her need to be closer to him overrode her need to stay connected to the kiss and she pulled back. 'Wet clothes suck.'

His laugh sent trails of delight shivering through her, which doubled in intensity as he hauled his T-shirt over his head, exposing a muscular chest and stomach with a smattering of dark hair trailing downwards and disappearing under the waistband of his shorts. She had to force breath into her lungs.

He held out his arms to her. 'Is this better?'

Better? He was a gift. Her gift. 'Almost.' Her gaze fell to his waist. 'But you're not completely unwrapped.'

'I will be in a moment.' He bent down to shuck his shorts.

She wanted to touch him, taste him and hold him against her, but she had to get her own clothes off first. Her fingers fumbled and her arms got tangled in cloying, wet cotton as she tried to drag her shirt over her head. Need duelled with frustration. The shirt finally came free and she managed to kick off her shorts. She tossed the soggy garments onto the bank next to Flynn's clothes and then reached down to unclasp her bra.

His hand covered hers, stalling her intent. 'I want to do that.'

She stared up into eyes as dark as polished jarrah. 'Really?'

He nodded almost hypnotically. 'Really.'

With a slow and deliberate touch he trailed the fingers of his free hand down along the ruched strap of her bra, across the lacy edges and down into the cleft between her breasts.

Her breasts strained against the soft fabric as each light caress fired off a volley of sensation, both delicious and tormenting at the same time.

His fingers undid the clasp with ease and with an almost reverent touch his hands cupped her breasts, supporting their tingling and aching weight.

'You're beautiful.' His thumb brushed her nipples.

A moan left her lips as her head fell back, her body quivering but demanding more.

With his hand on one breast, his mouth closed over the other, his heat roared through her like a fireball, torching every part of her and branding her as his.

Her legs buckled.

He pulled her against him and she wrapped her legs around his waist, feeling his desire for her hard and firm against her thigh. The wonder that she could arouse him showered over her, giving her a taste of power, and deep inside her a pulse throbbed.

She gave herself up to every glorious sensation, letting them rule her body and her mind, letting them drive out every fear and dread for the future, and letting them take her out of her normal world into a realm she couldn't have imagined existed.

The only thing that existed was his touch on her and selfishly she took it all.

He raised his head.

Don't stop, please, don't stop. Through the haze of desire she managed to focus on him. His eyes burned brightly with a fundamental craving. A craving for her.

She wrapped her arms around his neck and leaned forward, kissing him, seeking his essence and giving her own.

His palms gripped her buttocks, holding her close, and his chest shuddered against hers, his groan vibrating in her mouth. Then one hand slid between her thighs and his thumb caressed her.

Once.

Twice.

Thrice.

She shattered in a moment, crying out as sensation

ripped through her—giving, taking, changing. Creating a kernel of hope.

She sank against him, her head resting on his neck, embarrassment staining her cheeks. 'I'm sorry. Who knew I was this easy?'

'Shh.' He stroked her head, his voice soft. 'I wanted to give that to you. I don't want you to be sorry, I want you to be glad.'

Her heart soared in awe. She'd never had such a considerate lover.

He carried her through the water until his back was resting against the mossy bank. Holding her with one arm, he reached for his shorts.

She looked up over his shoulder. 'You came prepared?'

He grinned. 'One of us had to have a plan.' His fingers reached into his pocket.

She couldn't stop the wide smile breaking across her face. He'd wanted her as much as she'd wanted him. 'Good thinking. But I think it's my turn to give you something.' She plucked the small blue packet out of his hand.

'Hey!' He reached for it, his free hand wrapping around her wrist.

She quickly switched hands, knowing his other arm held her. 'I promise I'll be very thorough.'

He growled deep in his throat. 'That's what I'm worried about.' He suddenly let her go, grabbing the condom as she fell back, laughing.

The water slid over her as joy surged through her. She surfaced, still laughing. Flynn stood before her, tall and proud like a warrior ready for battle. Her laughter died in her throat as heady need exploded and muscles twitched, aching to be filled.

He hauled her against him, his breathing ragged, his eyes almost black with longing. Strong arms lifted her and she lowered herself onto him, taking him deeply with a hungry intensity that screamed to be sated.

'Flynn.' His name came out as a wail of longing.

It was all he needed.

He moved against her, filling her with heat, power and something undefinable. Something she didn't know she'd been missing.

On a maelstrom of sensation they climbed toward ecstasy, reaching it at the same moment in a blaze of lights that cascaded over them, sending them soaring beyond themselves, tempting them never to return.

The moon rose from behind a cloud, its bright white beams lighting the sky in a fair imitation of dawn. The frogs sang, the magpie geese honked and the fire crackled and hissed as Flynn sat with his back supported by a fallen tree. Mia rested between his legs; her back snuggled up against his chest and an unfamiliar feeling of contentment wove through him.

She tilted her head back and looked up at him, her eyes a smoky blue. 'I had no idea the bush was so noisy.'

He dropped a kiss onto her hair. 'Between the bright moon and those geese, I doubt we'll get much sleep tonight.'

She turned in his arms, her brows raised and her lips twitching with a smile. 'You were planning on sleeping, were you? I thought you might have had other plans.'

A swoop of desire meshed with laughter. 'You're going to wear me out.'

He couldn't believe his good fortune. He held an incredibly desirable woman in his arms, a woman who had made love to him with almost frenetic abandon in the waterhole and then gloriously slowly on the mossy bank, and she didn't want anything from him.

Something's not right.

He kicked the wayward thought straight out of his head, hard and fast, replacing it with the memory of how they'd lain together on a carpet of moss, exploring each other until the sinking sun and mosquitoes had forced them to retreat and make camp.

Her lips brushed his in a kiss devoid of heat but full of affection. 'I might need some food before I wear you out again. Do you think our seafood feast is ready?'

'It should be. The whelks have cooled and I'll check the barramundi.' He stood up, and hauled Mia to her feet. 'You get the plates.'

'Plastic or paper bark?'

'That's up to you. Paperbark plates just go into the fire at the end of the meal.'

She grinned. 'No washing-up suits me.' She flicked on her LED headlamp and walked over to a melaleuca tree to strip off some bark.

He unwrapped the fish and with a fork checked the flesh, which separated easily. He called to Mia, who was walking back toward him. 'Can you grab the sparkling grape juice and the salad out of the cooler?'

'Sure. How's my damper?'

'It's cooked and demanding lashings of butter.'

Five minutes later, with their paperbark plates filled with food, Flynn pulled a cooked whelk out of its shell and dangled it in front of Mia's mouth. 'Open wide.'

She pulled back slightly, a horrified look streaking across her face. 'It's bright blue.'

He loved teasing her. 'Yes, but at least it isn't moving, like the green ants.'

'True.' She sounded sceptical. 'What about I try a mussel first?'

He tucked a few stray stands of hair behind her ear. 'You're stalling.'

Indignation flared in her eyes and then laughter followed. 'You know me too well.'

'Hmm.' He smiled but her words snagged him. He really didn't know her very well at all because she played her cards so close to her chest.

'OK, here goes.' She leaned forward.

He dropped the snail into her open mouth and watched.

Her jaw moved up and down and then she swallowed. 'It's kind of like a leathery oyster but if I had my choice I prefer the barramundi.' She sipped her drink. 'I've always enjoyed fish. Dad used to take Michael and me fishing in a tinny and we'd catch flathead.'

Flynn took the mention of her brother as an invitation to find out more. 'Were you and you brother close?'

'We were close in age.' She broke open the damper, and steam rose into the night air. She sighed. 'I didn't see very much of him in the last couple of years after he moved to Melbourne.'

'Work?' Flynn ate a whelk himself, enjoying the strong flavour.

Mia busied herself with buttering the damper. 'Michael had been struggling for a while. He took a job in Melbourne to get away, to make a complete change.'

He wondered at her hesitation in answering. Why did she find it so very hard to talk about her family? 'Did the move help him?'

She raised her eyes to his, the moonlight reflecting her sadness. 'His death is listed as a car accident, which it was, but he was the sole occupant of the car. It ran off a straight stretch of road at four in the morning, hitting a tree.'

Code for suicide. As a doctor, Flynn knew that many single-vehicle accidents masked men who in the darkest hour of their depression decided to take their own lives. He put down his plate and wrapped his arms around her. 'Hell, Mia. I'm sorry.'

She shuddered against him. 'I should have done more, I should have gone over to visit him but I was—' Her voice stopped abruptly.

He stroked her hair, trying to soothe. 'You were taking care of your elderly mother.'

Her head shot up off his shoulder as if she'd been struck. She stared at him, her face pale and her expression shocked. 'How did you know that?'

Her accusatory tone surprised him. 'It's not that hard to work out, Mia. You're a nurse, a caring person, and your mum was unwell, so all the pieces of that story go together and lead to that conclusion.' He kissed her cheek, wondering at her reaction. 'It's not a state secret, is it?'

She dropped her gaze and sat back. 'No, sorry, of course it isn't.' She scooped up her plate and picked up a chunk of fish. 'Talking of state secrets, I've wanted to know for ages, why do they call you turtle man?'

He knew she'd just deliberately changed the subject and he shouldn't let her, but he didn't want to push and ruin a perfect day and soon-to-be perfect night. He rested his hand on the back of her neck. 'You realise, if I tell you, I might have to kill you or at the very least extract some sort of payment.'

'I'm willing to take the risk.'

Her husky laugh raced through him like Kirra wild-fires. 'I see you're the type of woman who likes to live on the edge.'

Her laughter, so freely given, faded quickly and she turned to take a drink, but not before he'd caught a glimpse of stark resignation in her eyes. She turned back and smiled almost too brightly. 'Right now I'm living for the moment.' She suddenly lunged at him, her hands finding his ribs and meting out a severe tickling.

Any disquiet he had about her was lost in a sea of mirth and aching ribs. He finally wrapped his arms around her and caught his breath, breathing in the minute traces of her perfume that had somehow with-stood the combination of water and mud.

He rested his chin on the top of her head. 'As a kid, one of my strongest memories of my time on Kirra was coming to North Point. I'd lie in the dunes and watch the turtles lumber up from the sea, digging their nesting holes in the sand and laying their eggs. It was the most awesome sight.'

He chuckled as the memories came back. 'I used to try and convince the Kirra kids that they shouldn't eat the eggs and they used to look at me as if I was stark, raving mad. When I came back to Kirra as an adult, one of the first things I did was help get a wildlife programme off the ground that tracks the Olive Ridley turtles.'

She trailed her fingers along the back of his hand, sending his blood pounding.

'And they gave you the name of turtle man.'

'That's right.'

She snuggled closer to him, and shot him a cheeky look. 'So you're telling me I can't serve turtle eggs to Susie and the crew tomorrow night even though that is the one thing I can find without too much trouble?'

He wound a strand of her hair around his finger, rising to her seductive teasing with a bit of his own. 'Well, you could but there are saltwater crocodiles in the ocean and they're quite happy to charge up the beach to take a pretty RAN.'

Her squeal of horror filled him with delight.

She turned, resting on her knees and wrapping her arms around his neck. 'How about tomorrow you shoot me a goose? By the sounds of all the honking there's a huge flock down on the billabong. I'll cook it with melaleuca leaves, which will give it a lemon flavour.'

'Great idea.' He rested his forehead on hers. 'I've got another great idea.'

'Have you?'

Her fingers trailed through his hair, coaxing and luring.

'I have. One that involves a full moon, a fire and a swag.'

Her lips curved upwards in a slow and sultry smile. 'I like the way you think.'

His banked desire for her flared, reducing all thoughts to ash. But he didn't need to think with this amazing woman in his arms because he knew exactly what he wanted to do and it started with a kiss.

Mia tied off the rubbish bag and headed outside to dump it in the disposal unit. Thunder rumbled teasingly in the distance as it had done for days, and on the horizon a vivid white scar of lightning jagged across the dusk sky. The dry season was coming to an end and the humidity had reached breaking point, but still the rain hadn't come. Yet.

She mopped her forehead with a small hand towel that rested on her shoulder for that purpose. The wet air gave no relief to the heat and every day she virtually 'steamed'. Between the humidity, the sandflies and the skin fungal infections, everyone was itchy and scratchy. No wonder they called this pre-wet the 'troppo' season. Susie and Jenny had been busy with their 'strong women' group and closely monitoring people with depression, making sure they took their medication.

She headed back inside to turn off the lights and head home. *Home to Flynn?* She glanced at her watch and gave herself a good shake. *No expectations, remember.* Time meant nothing to Flynn and today he'd been out on the west side of the island. Chances were he'd stay for a campfire meal and some dancing. Besides, her house wasn't his home, although, for the last few weeks when he'd been in Kirra, he'd been cooking in her kitchen, relaxing on her couch and sleeping in her bed, his arms wrapped snugly around her.

Since their campout they'd only been apart when

he'd been working on the other islands. She smiled at the treasured memory of their wonderful two days in the bush. The love-making had been spectacular but her most treasured times had been spending the day gathering and preparing the meal for Susie and company. They'd talked and laughed and cheerfully argued over the state of the coals and how long it took to cook the magpie goose.

It had been a huge success and Susie had even complimented her on her yams. It had been a consolation time with the indigenous health workers and now they were a solid team. Right now, life was good.

Life is good because of Flynn.

No. Life was good because she was taking one day at a time and embracing the time she had left before her behaviour became more impulsive, before she struggled for words, before her concentration failed her and she had to give up work and leave Kirra.

Flynn was just for now. Flynn was part of 'one day at a time'.

She did the final lockdown check and slung her bag over her shoulder.

'Miss!'

She glanced up to see a young girl running toward her, holding a bundle, and a few steps behind her a man followed, his step brisk, his expression anxious.

Mia hurried over, her brain running through a list of possible medical dramas. 'Is there something wrong?'

Wide green eyes brimming with tears looked up at her. 'Can you help?' The girl shoved the bundle at Mia.

Mia peeled back outer layer of the bundle to find a tiny

baby joey nestled inside a pink windcheater. Surprise mingled with awe. 'Oh. But I'm a nurse, not a vet.'

'We're terribly sorry.' The man spoke. 'It's the last hour of our holiday and the plane's leaving shortly. Megan found the Joey and the store told us there's no vet on the island so we thought perhaps you could take care of it.'

'Please.' Megan put her hands together. 'I can't leave until I know he's going to be all right.'

Mia looked at the young girl's hopeful expression and her father's expectant smile. She knew nothing about raising wildlife. The joey wriggled, its brown eyes staring up at her, and something inside her melted. 'Sure, leave him with me and I'll do my best.'

'Thank you so much.' Relief rushed across Megan's father's face. 'Come on, Megs, we have to catch this plane.' He caught his daughter's hand and urged her to walk back to the car.

Meg started to walk away and then turned back, calling, 'Can I email the clinic and ask you to send me photos?'

Mia nodded and waved, still rather bewildered by the last few minutes.

Just as she turned to go back into the clinic, Flynn's truck pulled up. He swung out of the vehicle, and walked toward her, a wide smile on his face.

The now familiar streak of delight she experienced every time she saw him spun through her, weaving its promise of magical times.

His arm slid around her waist as his lips stole a kiss. 'Hello. What have you got there?' He stared down at the bundle in her arms.

'A joey.'

'So I see. They need to be kept tucked up like they're still in the pouch.' His tanned fingers nestled the windcheater warmly around the tiny marsupial. 'Ah, night feeds, twice-daily oiling, pouch changing and weighing.' He looked up and grinned. 'I think you just became a mother.'

A mother. Her head spun as her blood rushed to her feet. The two simple words sliced through her with stinging intensity, bringing her real world thundering back. The real world she'd kept at bay these last few weeks with Flynn.

She would never be able to be a mother.

'Hey, you OK? You've gone all pale.' His fingers stroked her face.

She nodded, taking a moment to find her voice, not wanting him to guess. 'I'm fine.' She forced the muscles of her face to smile. 'It's just the surprise of it all. I've no idea how to care for this little guy.'

'No problem. I've raised a joey before and I'm happy to help. We've got infant formula and I'm sure you've got something to make a baby sling tucked away in that magic cupboard of yours. The one that produces all sorts of wild and wonderful things.'

He winked at her, his eyes crinkling with a wonderfully, caring smile, tinged with heat. 'I'll even share the night feeds with you if you bake me some of that wonderful bread of yours.'

This is what it would be like if you had a child with Flynn.

The wound on her heart tore wide open. She could

never have a child. She could never risk passing on the awful mutant gene on chromosome seventeen. Never, ever.

Take one day at a time. Don't think further than today. With strength she hadn't known she had, she pushed her pain back down deep, sealing it away and covering it with teasing. 'I think some fresh bread could be arranged if you do the three a.m. shift.'

'Three a.m.?' His brows rose to his hairline in mock effrontery. 'I was thinking more like midnight.'

'I guess it depends how much you really want that bread.' Still protecting the joey, she leaned in and captured his mouth with hers, her tongue quickly stealing his taste and giving some of her own.

His eyes darkened and he cleared his throat. 'Three a.m. will be just fine.'

She laughed. 'I thought you'd see it my way.'

His hand tightened on her waist and he steered her toward the clinic. 'Come on, this is going to be fun.'

CHAPTER NINE

RAIN pounded the windows, running down the glass in huge streams, faster than the wipers could clear the windscreen. The wet had finally arrived and at three o'clock every day the heavens opened, the rain bucketing down hard and fast for an hour and then stopping as abruptly as it had started.

Flynn ran the short distance from the truck to Mia's back door, but he arrived sopping wet. He kicked off his boots and grabbed a towel from the pile Mia had put by the door. 'Anyone home?'

'I'm in here.' Mia's voice called from the living room.

He followed the melodic sound and saw her before she saw him. Semi-reclining on the couch with her long, golden legs fully stretched out, she had the pouch nestled against her chest and was feeding 'Joe', the bottle tilted confidently in her hand. Joe's little mouth was sucking overtime, his small cheeks moving inwards while Mia gazed down at him, her expression soft and full of affection.

An image of her holding a baby rocked through him.

His baby. He waited for the feeling of abject horror to scald him. It didn't come.

'Oh, hi, you're back early.' Mia looked up and smiled but then a frown formed three creases on the bridge of her nose. 'Tell me you didn't land in this rain.'

'I keep telling you that planes are safer than cars but, no, I got in just ahead of the rain.' He leaned over and kissed her. 'How's our boy?'

'He's doing fine and he's grown so much in the three days since you last saw him. And he loves it when I hang his pouch on the door and he can watch the world go by.'

'Excellent. He'll be ready to have some time out of the pouch soon.' He chucked the joey under the chin. 'Ah, kids, they grow up so fast.'

'You sound like a father.' Mia put the now empty bottle on the coffee-table and stood up. She headed into the bathroom and helped Joe toilet before she returned to the couch with the little marsupial curled up in his sling pouch, his feet sticking up around his head.

She looked like a serene mother, at one with her role as a nurturer.

Flynn rested his thigh on the top of the couch and ran his hand through Mia's hair, having missed touching her for the last two nights. 'Have you thought about it?'

She glanced up at him, her blue eyes vivid and questioning. 'Thought about what?'

'About being a mother.'

She seemed to shudder under his hand and he heard a soft gasp.

'As I don't plan to get married, I guess that means I'm not going to have children.'

His fingers traced her ear. 'Many women do it on their own.'

'I'm not many women.' She gave him a penetrating look. 'And I think both of us know what it's like, missing one parent in the "growing-up" stakes. I wouldn't wish that on a child.'

'True.' But sadness curled around his heart. 'I think it's a shame you won't rethink the marriage thing. You have so much to offer and you'd make a great mother.'

Her brows rose high and her eyes widened in surprise. Then she blinked and cleared her throat. 'I could say the same thing about you.'

He grinned and deliberately misconstrued her comment. 'I'd never be a great mother.'

Her mouth flattened and she pushed Joe's pouch into his arms. 'Ha-ha. You know I meant you rethinking the marriage thing. Brooke was *one* woman.' She stood up and walked around to him, her hand resting gently on his forearm. 'I know she hurt you but there are women out there who can make you happy, but you'll never know if you stay on Kirra. You need to get out there and meet them.'

Why was she pushing this? 'I have no desire or need to leave Kirra.' *No desire to leave you.* The idea socked him hard. The last couple of months had been the most content he'd ever been and he wanted to hold onto that.

He didn't want to spend time talking about what Mia thought was best for him. He didn't want her pushing him back to the mainland and the dating scene.

I don't expect you to marry me, I don't expect or want anything from you. Mia's words reinforced his plans.

There was no reason for things to change. In fact, he just wanted things to stay exactly the way they were. Easy, relaxed and spectacularly sexy.

He slung Joe's sling across his chest so the joey rested against his hip. 'Come on. The rain's easing. Let's take Joe and go for a drive to North Point. We can park and watch the sun set.'

She stood in front of him, beautiful and vibrant with an unreadable expression. Then she smiled and stepped into his arms. 'I'm not sure how I feel about making out in front of an impressionable joey.'

'I'll pack him a mask.' He pulled her close and kissed her.

Mia watched Flynn as they drove toward North Point. She could gaze at him for hours, watching how the tendons on his hands rippled over his knuckles, how his innate strength radiated along his jaw, and how his eyes sparkled every time he looked at her.

She wanted to bottle the feeling that sizzled inside her when he smiled so she could keep it for ever. Keep it with her when she left. Or when he left. She knew they were on borrowed time. But she wanted to die knowing he was happy and settled. She wanted him to find a woman to love but each time she brought up the subject he resisted.

And why was he asking her about having children? They were having an affair, pure and simple.

Except it was far from simple.

She'd noticed he'd recently been doing day trips to Burra and Mugur whenever it was possible and reducing the number of nights he was away. His razor and tooth-brush were in her bathroom cabinet and she doubted he had many clothes left in his own wardrobe. He hadn't slept at his place in weeks.

Not that she minded. She loved going to sleep in the security of his arms every night. He was the first person she thought of when she woke up and the last person she thought of when she closed her eyes at night.

I think it's a shame you won't rethink the marriage thing. His words unsettled her. Surely he wasn't re-thinking the idea of an affair, thinking about making it something more permanent?

You're over thinking this. Just take it one day at a time.

Flynn slung his arm over her shoulder, drawing her closer. 'You're very quiet.'

She shuffled across the bench seat, her shoulder resting under his. 'I'm just admiring the view.'

He glanced at her, slightly bemused. 'It's just scrub. We haven't got to the coast yet.'

She rested her hand on his thigh. 'I'm talking about you.'

Heat surged through him as his blood pounded faster. Her touch did that do him every, single time. He could never get enough of it.

She sighed. 'I do enjoy North Point but do you know what I really miss?'

'What?'

'I miss strolling along the beach at sunset, trailing my feet through the water.'

He grimaced. 'At the best of times it's not safe but at this time of year the crocodiles are really territorial and will attack without warning. Plus they're on the move too because the wet gives them a lot more waterways to traverse than the dry.'

She shivered. 'Watching the sunset from the top of the cliff is just fine.'

He grinned. 'I thought you'd agree with me.' He took a left turn and slowed as he drove through a small community.

The road was raised over three huge drains that diverted a creek under the road. The coffee-brown, muddy, wet-season waters poured through the drains and back into the creek.

'Oh, no, look at that.' Mia pointed through the windscreen. The children of the community were using the drain overflow as a waterslide and diving pool. 'Heaven knows what sort of diseases they're going to pick up from that. Gastro at the very least.'

He braked and pulled over. 'I'll tell them to get out.'

Mia reached for the door handle and smiled. 'I'll do it. It's your turn to give Joe a pit stop so he doesn't soil his pouch.'

He laughed. 'Fair enough.'

The squeals of delighted kids riding the natural waterslide drifted in the air as Mia walked over to them.

Flynn gently removed Joe from the pouch and squatted down over the red dirt and stimulated his cloacal area with a damp tissue.

Joe happily obliged and urinated and defecated neatly. Flynn gave him a quick rub behind the ears and returned him to the pouch, suspending him from the interior hook that hung from the handle over the door.

He heard Mia talking to the children, her voice cheerful and laughing.

Planning to head over to her, he walked around the back of the truck just as a child jumped from the road into the waterhole.

He shielded his eyes against the low sun and had taken three steps when he caught sight of a long, rough, olive coloured log sliding out of the large drain.

He started. That didn't seem right. A log that size would surely have been caught and stuck further up in the drains. He did a double-take and caught the flash of yellow menacing eyes.

'Crocodile,' Flynn yelled as loudly as he could.

At the same moment Mia screamed. '*Yirrikipayi!* Get out of the water now!'

The children frantically scrambled up the muddy sides of the creek but one little girl froze, staring straight at the crocodile.

Flynn raced back to the truck, frantically fitting the key into the lock of the gun box. 'Come on, open.'

Mia scooped up two discarded cans and threw them at the reptile.

The lock opened and Flynn grabbed the gun, and immediately started running back toward the creek.

The crocodile's tail flicked slowly back and forth, its back humped and rising out of the water. One nostril flared.

Mia darted a quick look at Flynn as he approached. A look identical to the one she'd given him seconds before she'd thrown herself out of the truck and into the path of Joel and his gun. His inhaled breath stalled, trapped in his throat. He knew with horrendous clarity what she planned to do.

'Mia, no!'

But his shouted plea did nothing and his heart threatened to stop.

She leapt into the water between the child and the beast, catching the child under the arms and throwing her to safety.

Mia's rapid movements would provoke the crocodile to attack. Flynn raised his gun, he had to save her.

I love her.

He had to save the woman he loved as much as life itself. She had to live so he could tell her how much he loved her.

Breathing hard against his fear, he gripped the gun firmly, as much to steady it as to keep his hands from shaking. He lined up the sights, praying he could hit the beast and disorient it. Praying he would completely miss Mia.

He had to get this right.

The brown water suddenly churned white and the crocodile lunged just as Mia hurled herself sideways. Its jaw missed her torso, instead clamping down on her left arm. It immediately started to roll, intending to pull her down under the water and drown her.

Her scream of terror rent the air as she plunged her fingers into its eyes.

Now! Flynn pulled the trigger, aiming for the crocodile's hips, the sound of the gun deafening but not loud enough to silence Mia's scream.

The bullet hit its back and the crocodile thrashed, its jaw slackening.

Mia flung herself onto the bank, her arms and legs slipping in the mud as she struggled for purchase.

The reptile swam toward her and jumped for her legs.

Flynn aimed for its head and fired.

The bullet hit the side of the head and it fell back into the water with a loud splash, its three-metre length slowly sinking.

Thank you. Thank you. Relief poured through him but adrenaline kept him centred because the battle wasn't over yet. Her arm looked like a mangled mess.

He ran to Mia, pulling her away from the creek bank, pulling her into his arms. 'I thought I'd lost you.' His hands ran all over her, checking her, as if touching made him believe she was still alive.

Her shaking, wet body trembled in his arms and her head bobbed up and down, her teeth chattering so hard she couldn't talk.

His palms cradled her face, forcing her to look at him. 'Don't *ever* do anything like that to me again, do you hear me?' He kissed her forehead and held her tight. 'I couldn't bear to lose you, Mia.'

Blank, sky-blue eyes stared up at him, devoid of emotion. Devoid of the vital life force he associated so much with Mia. Dread tore at him. He'd just rescued the woman he loved from the jaws of a crocodile, but for a split second he had an insidious feeling that the prehistoric beast wasn't their biggest predator.

He pulled off his shirt, ripping it into long strips while he gave himself a shake, cross that he would listen to crazy intuition that was completely wrong. The look in her eyes was just shock. The same thing had happened after Joel.

People came running from everywhere, having heard the shots and the cries. Robbo's police vehicle pulled up and the policeman jumped out.

'I shot a three-metre salty, Robbo. You can charge me later. Check the kids and look after Joe for me. Right now I've got to get Mia to the clinic.'

The stunned policeman shook his head. 'No charge, Flynn. Self-defence, mate. You look after Mia. I'll look after this mob.' He jerked his head to the gathering crowd.

Mia's lacerated arm hung limply by her side, bleeding and floppy, the humerus obviously broken. Flynn wrapped the cotton lengths firmly around the lacerated skin, creating a makeshift compression bandage. He was second-guessing the extent of the damage. He was certain of muscle and tendon injuries and there was a high chance the crocodile's teeth could have punctured an artery or vein, causing internal bleeding.

Mia stayed silent, her eyes following his every move. With the last piece of his shirt he created a collar and cuff sling. 'I'm taking you to the clinic now. You're going to be fine, sweetheart.'

She nodded but remained silent, her expression vacant.

Fear clawed at him as he swung her into his arms, carrying her to the truck. Where was his vibrant Mia? It was like she'd disappeared and left a shell behind. He tucked a towel around her shivering body before closing the door and running around to the driver's side, not wanting to leave her alone for a second.

She hadn't spoken a word since the attack and he was frantic to examine her. Frantic to get her to Darwin and under the care of a plastic surgeon. With one hand holding her right hand and the other gripping the steering-wheel, he gunned the engine and sped down the gravel road.

Mia felt Flynn's strong arms lifting her out of the truck. She let her head lie on his shoulder, feeling his heart beating under her chest, feeling his arms secure around her. Trying to focus on that and push away the image of jagged teeth and yellow eyes.

Flynn had saved her life.

Her wonderful crocodile hunter, the man she loved, had killed the prey that had threatened her. *But he can't kill the other prey.*

She couldn't stop shaking. She couldn't get her mouth to work. She felt like she was floating outside her body, watching the events around her. Her thoughts jumbled through her head, everything that had happened in the last half-hour a hazy and disconnected blur. Her arm throbbed with pain, which she welcomed because at least that meant some nerves were still attached.

'Lie down.' He laid her on the examination table and went to the top cupboard.

She struggled up onto her good elbow, finally finding her voice. 'The saline's in the lower cupboard and the antibiotics are—'

Flynn spun around, his face grim. 'Lie down, Mia. You're the patient, so behave,' he growled as he grabbed the equipment he needed.

'Will I lose my arm?' She blurted out the words, half wanting to know, the other half of her preferring not to know.

'Not if I can help it.' He picked up the satellite phone, dialled a number and tucked it under his ear. 'You're going to Darwin for the best care possible. I want a plastic surgeon to operate.'

She bit her lip against her shaking, grateful for his care.

She listened to him order the air ambulance while he wrapped the blood-pressure cuff around her uninjured arm.

The phone call ended and he put the phone down next to her and pumped up the cuff. As he released the value his brow creased in concentration and concern. 'One hundred on sixty.'

The image of horned eyebrows and a long snout thundered through her and paralysing fear gripped her. *Think about now. Think about your treatment.* 'Perhaps it just broke my arm.'

'Perhaps.' He touched her hand. 'It's cool but that could be due to my pressure bandage.' He slid the tourniquet up her arm and swabbed her hand. 'As soon as I've put this IV in, I'm going to do an ultrasound to check your brachial artery. If there's bleeding I'm going to have to do a fasciotomy to release the pressure.'

She nodded her understanding. She knew all the theory and she tried to focus on that. *IV, ultrasound, evacuation, Theatre.* She silently said the words over and over as she watched him guide the cannula into the back of her hand.

But snapshot images started exploding in her head.

Colour images. Moving images. Images so real she was in them.

The little girl frozen with terror.

The crocodile's hunched back. The intent in his un-blinking eyes.

The crunching sound as its jaw snapped down hard on her arm.

Her throat closed, she couldn't breathe. She hadn't thought about herself, she'd just jumped to save the little girl who would have died instantly.

Impulse. Twice in four months she'd done something stupid and thoughtless. It was starting. The dementia that haunted her family was starting and she couldn't ignore it any more.

She grabbed Flynn's arm, staring up at him, panic tearing at her. 'I couldn't let her die.' Words tumbled out over each other. 'She's too little to die. I'm going to die anyway but when the croc got me I didn't want to die, but I will and I can't stop it.'

Flynn's startled expression soon changed to one of unflappable calm. He stroked her hair, his voice soothing. 'You're safe now, Mia, you're not going to die. We're going to save your arm and after a few days in hospital everything will be fine.'

Hysteria gripped her and tears cascaded down her cheeks. She shook her head, her voice rising. 'No, you don't understand. I'm going to die. I know I'm going to die.'

He pressed his lips against her forehead. 'Shh, this is post-traumatic stress talking and I'm going to give you something to calm you down and make you sleep.'

He wiped her tears away with the soft pads of his thumb. 'I didn't save you so I could lose you. Everything is going to be all right. I promise that you and I are going to have a long life and grow old together.'

I didn't save you so I could lose you.

Intense pain unlike anything she'd ever experienced before dragged through her, hard, sharp and devastating. He loved her but she was lost to him already. She tried to speak but she couldn't move air in or out of her chest.

She saw Flynn reach for the oxygen mask as blackness rolled in from the edges of her mind. Then his image faded as the darkness swamped her completely.

CHAPTER TEN

MIA squinted against the light that crept in though the slatted blinds, illuminating her eyelids and waking her up. She automatically tried to turn to check her bedside clock, wondering what time it was.

Red-hot pain seared her. She glanced to her left and saw her arm suspended in a sling, hanging from a pole next to the bed. The back of her right hand contained an intravenous drip, which was attached to a pump. Her mouth tasted of metal, her skin smelt of Betadine, her head felt fuzzy and her hair lay in clumps lank against the pillow.

Hospital.

She had no recollection of arriving. She didn't remember much at all except being held in Flynn's arms after the attack. She shuddered and immediately pushed the thoughts away. She didn't want to relive yesterday at all.

'You're awake?' Flynn's warm lips caressed her cheek. 'How are you feeling?'

The warmth in his voice and lips rolled through her and she reached up, touching his cheek, reassuring herself that he was real and she was fine. 'Just peachy.' Her voice croaked through her dry mouth. 'Can I have drink, please?'

'Sure.' He poured water into a glass from a plastic jug and with a dextrous flick angled the straw. Then he gently eased her upward and pushed another pillow behind her back so she was half-reclined and handed her the glass, steadying the straw against her lips.

The water tasted cold and sweet and she gulped it down. 'Thanks. You'd make a good nurse.'

He sat down on the bed facing her, his eye's twinkling. 'I learned from the best.'

Her lips curved upwards. 'Flattery will get you everywhere.'

He grinned. 'That's the plan.'

She wriggled her fingers of her left hand just to test they worked. Relief filled her. 'I don't really remember too much after you put me in the truck.'

Flynn picked up her uninjured hand, gently stroking her fingers. 'After I got you back to the clinic you started to hyperventilate, which is pretty understandable after what you'd just been through. I gave you some diazepam to calm you down and that helped slow down your bleeding.'

'Sorry.' She squeezed his hand. 'I don't remember flipping out.'

'That's OK. It's all part of the job.' His eyes stared into hers, their hazel depths brimming with care and affection. 'The air ambulance arrived and you were pretty drowsy on the flight. Simon Peters, the plastic surgeon, met us in A and E and you went straight to Theatre.'

She stared up at her arm, which was swathed in layers and layers of white gauze bandage. She couldn't remember anything about going to Theatre. 'How's my circulation?'

Flynn reached over and touched the fingers on her injured arm. 'Toasty warm and pink, so I'd say your circulation is perfect.' He pulled her chart off the end of the bed and passed it to her. 'See for yourself.

'The staff checked it all night and there haven't been any concerns. Simon said the repair went well and he doesn't anticipate any problems. You have about three hundred tiny stitches but no skin grafts were required.'

He pointed to the drug order. 'The biggest worry is the risk of a Pseudomonas infection from the water or the teeth so you're on strong antibiotics, which might make you feel a bit nauseous.'

Her stomach rolled. 'I think that's already happening.'

He tilted his head thoughtfully. 'You might be hungry. It's been a long time since you ate.'

She grimaced. 'Oh, great, a week of hospital food. I can't wait.'

'Well, I've got some news that might make you smile.' Again his gaze rested on hers, his eyes shining with a light she'd not seen before. It puzzled her because she thought she knew his every look and expression.

'Simon is happy to discharge you into my care tomorrow morning. I've got us a suite at The Gardens, overlooking the harbour where we can spend the week before you have your post-op appointment with Simon in his rooms. You can relax, read and enjoy some pampering.'

His unexpected words stunned her. 'But what about work? Kirra needs their doctor.'

He smiled down at her indulgently, as if she was an innocent child who didn't understand how the world worked. 'I've organised to take some annual leave and Northern Territory Health has sent in two relievers to cover for both of us.'

She couldn't stop herself from frowning, which was crazy because she should be happy. She should be thrilled that he wanted to do this for her but something inside her rebelled against his words. She didn't understand the feeling but it forced her to speak. 'But you don't want to lose a week of your annual leave looking after me. You should be saving that for going south for a real break because this will be like a busman's holiday. I'll be fine here, truly.'

The crinkly smile lines around his eyes smoothed. 'I'm not going to leave you here alone for a week.' He raised her right hand to his mouth, and pressed his lips against her fingers. 'In fact, I'm not planning on ever leaving you.'

I promise that you and I are going to have a long life and grow old together.

Her breath swooped out of her lungs as her memory flooded back. Yesterday at the clinic. His tenderness. The words he'd spoken that had told her that he loved her.

And now he'd just told her again.

Flynn loved her.

And she loved him with every part of her.

A silent cry ripped through her. This wasn't supposed to have happened. It was supposed to have been an affair. He was supposed to get over Brooke with her and then meet someone, fall in love and head off to have a long and happy life with a household full of children.

He shouldn't love her. She couldn't give him those things.

He couldn't love her, she wouldn't let him.

Flynn wasn't like Steven and when he found out about the frontotemporal dementia he would not abandon her. He would insist on staying and caring for her. But he deserved so much more than being tied down, watching her disappear behind the wall of dementia until she was mute and a wasted shadow of herself.

She'd always known one of them would leave the affair first. Today she knew it would be her.

Flynn had showered, shaved and rung the ward. Twice. The first time he'd been told Mia was in the shower, and the second time that Simon Peters was talking to her.

He ached to see her but he'd given up pacing and waiting. Instead he'd gone shopping to fill in the time until eleven a.m. He'd loaded the fridge with fresh fruit, vegetables, gourmet cheeses and bakery-fresh bread, the likes of which Kirra had never seen. He'd bought flowers, chocolates and six magazines because he had no idea which ones Mia would enjoy the most, and he'd also purchased a best-selling novel that the woman in the bookshop had recommended.

On the way back from the bookshop he'd passed a jewellery store. Usually the sight of sparkling diamonds and gold chains was enough to force him to cross the street, but today he'd found himself studying rings and wondering what type of engagement ring Mia would want. He could picture an emerald, diamond and sapphire combination, which depicted the colours of Kirra, the place they had met.

After everything he'd been through with Brooke he'd never expected to want to propose again or marry anyone, but Mia had altered that. Mia, with her zest for life, her teasing smile and understanding ways, had come into his life and changed it for ever. And yesterday, when he'd come so close to losing her, he'd known right there and then he was never letting her go.

When he picked up Mia from hospital at eleven o'clock, that signalled the start of their new life together. He couldn't wait. He glanced at his watch and grabbed his keys. His heart kicked up a beat. It was time to go.

Ten minutes later he stepped out of the lift into the ward. Surgical wards were busy places on weekday mornings. White-coated residents strode purposefully, conducting ward rounds and pre-theatre examinations. Porters negotiated trolleys through narrow doorways and cheerfully greeted anxious patients with a joke and a smile, and nursing staff walked as quickly as they could, stopping just short of breaking into a run as they administered pre-medications, attended to wound care, and listened to patients' fears and concerns.

Flynn made his way down the long corridor, dodging all the action of the morning, and smiled at he passed a couple making their way slowly down the ward. The man held an overnight bag and flowers in one hand and his other hand rested gently on the seated woman's shoulder as a nurse pushed her wheelchair toward the lift. The relief and joy on their faces was clear for all to see. The hospital stay was behind them and they were going home.

That would be him and Mia in five minutes. He walked toward the door of the private room where he'd kissed Mia goodnight the previous evening. He pushed down the large, metal doorhandle and as he opened the door he joked, 'I've come to take you away, yah, ha!'

'You can take me anywhere you like, handsome.' An elderly woman with a blue rinse and a crocheted bed-jacket sat up in bed and gave him a toothless grin.

Flynn stopped abruptly, completely stunned. 'You're not Mia.'

'Sweet boy, if I was fifty years younger I bet I could be.' The woman chuckled. 'So who's this Mia I'm in competition with?'

He found himself grinning a wide, crazy smile. 'I hope by this afternoon she'll be my fiancée.'

'Ah, young love! She's a lucky girl.'

'Thank you.' He smiled his 'doctor smile', the one he used for flirty, elderly women. 'But if I were a free man, things would be different.'

'Oh, get on with you. Off you go and find your girl.' She lifted her arm and shooed him away.

Flynn hurried to the nurses' station to ask which room Mia was in, but found it deserted, with the phone ringing. He peered at the patient board but couldn't see Mia's name.

Bridgette, the unit nurse manager, rushed past and smiled in recognition as she reached for the phone. 'Morning, Doc, did Mia forget something?'

Forget something? He had no idea what she was talking about. He drummed his fingers on the desk as he waited impatiently for the nurse to finish her call. He'd wanted to be walking out the door with Mia right about now.

The moment Bridgette hung up the phone he spoke. 'Which room have you moved Mia to?'

'Moved her to?' Genuine bewilderment crossed the nurse's freckled face. 'But she left half an hour ago with you.'

He shook his head. 'No, she didn't. I just arrived to collect her.'

Two frown lines creased between her eyes. 'But when I gave Mia her discharge medications she told me that you'd gone to hail a taxi to bring it around to the front entrance.'

Why would she have said that? Had she been so keen to leave the ward and the hospital that she'd thought she'd wait for him downstairs even though she'd known he was coming at eleven? He'd walked right through the uncrowded entrance and he would have seen her if she'd been waiting for him there.

A vision of Mia collapsed somewhere in the hospital thundered through him. 'You didn't let her leave the hospital unescorted, did you?' The words shot out accusingly.

Bridgette visibly bristled. 'No, Doctor, I most certainly did not. We followed protocol to a T. Simon Peters had just finished his discharge examination and as he was heading downstairs anyway, he offered to escort her to you and the car.'

'Then where the hell is she?' His voice started to rise

as a sliver of dread crawled through him. 'What did she write on the discharge form?'

Bridgette pulled the history from the pile. '"The Gardens." Ooh, nice place.'

Thoughts jumbled in his head. None of this was making sense. 'Get Simon Peters on the ward phone and ask him where he left Mia.' He flipped open his own phone and rang the reception of The Gardens. Mia hadn't checked in. No one answered the phone in their room. Finally, he slapped his phone shut.

'Simon's on the line.' Bridgette held out the ward phone's handset to Flynn, apprehension stark on her face.

He almost snatched it from her hand. 'Simon, Flynn Harrington.'

'Flynn, mate, everything all right? Have you got the gorgeous Mia resting in a cocoon of luxury?' The plastic surgeon's bonhomie boomed down the line.

Flynn breathed in deeply, trying to keep his voice calm. 'Actually, that's what I'm ringing about. I've come to collect Mia and she isn't here. Bridgette said you took her downstairs to meet me, but at that point I hadn't even arrived. Into whose care did you leave her?'

'I thought I was leaving her with you.' There was a slight hesitation before Simon continued. 'As we arrived at the front entrance I got a page to return to the ward. Mia told me she could see a taxi coming and it was probably you. She insisted I go back upstairs to see the patient. Are you sure she isn't at The Gardens?'

Flynn ran his hand through his hair. 'I've checked and she's not there.'

'I'm sorry, Flynn.' Genuine regret sounded in his

voice. 'She didn't give me any indication that she was going anywhere other than to The Gardens with you.'

Flynn rang off, the sliver of dread expanding into a chasm. 'She's got into a taxi and disappeared into thin air. Hell, she could be unconscious somewhere.'

Bridgette shook her head. 'In the unlikely event that she collapsed in a taxi between here and The Gardens, the driver would have brought her straight back. Ring them again. You might have just crossed paths and by now she's ensconced on the bed, resting.'

He wanted so much to believe Bridgette but most of him kept asking, *Why didn't she wait for me?* He redialled the hotel and asked Reception to go and check if Mia was in the room. He paced back and forth, waiting on hold until he was told the room was vacant. He rang off. 'She's not there.'

'Oh.' The small word was spoken slowly and was loaded with meaning.

Ignoring her, he grabbed a pen and scrawled his mobile number on a piece of paper, agitation making the numbers blur. He shoved it at Bridgette. 'If she contacts the ward, ring me on my mobile straight away. I'm going to go the police.'

'Flynn, she's not missing.'

'Yes, she is!'

The unit manager jumped at his yell but held her ground. 'I know you're upset but…' She reached out and put her hand gently onto his forearm. 'Can you think of any reason why she didn't want to go to The Gardens with you?'

Didn't want to go with you.

His blood instantly drained to his feet as the roar of organ music swelled in his head. Music that had played for over an hour while he'd waited for a bride that had never shown. Music that had played in a shopping centre while he'd waited for his mother who had never appeared.

Mia wasn't missing. With no note and with no warning, Mia had gone.

He threw off Bridgette's hand, spun on his heel and almost ran from the ward. His feet took him into the lift, out across the entrance with its decorated floor, and into the steaming humidity. He passed the taxi rank without stopping, barely noticing the tropical palms and attractive gardens. He kept walking, not caring where he was going as long as he was moving.

He saw a juice container in the gutter and with a bellow he swung his leg back and then brought it forward, kicking the bottle hard, relishing the release it gave him. A woman walking along the footpath quickly grabbed her pre-schooler's hand and crossed the road.

He turned into a park and took a long drink from a water fountain then slumped onto a bench, sweat pouring down his neck. He rested his head in his hands, catching his breath.

How had he been so stupid? Why had he let down his guard?

He knew better. Hell, for two years he'd avoided relationships for good reason. Women left him. It was what they did. First his mother, then Brooke. And now Mia had abandoned him.

He knew better than to trust a woman. They took his

love and then they walked away, trampling his heart with their receding footsteps. Every single time.

How had he let a pair of amazing blue eyes, long blonde hair and the tantalising scent of Mia derail him?

Because there is so much more to Mia than that.

The thought burned into him, stilling his tumultuous and churning mind. He sat up, his hand gripping the edge of the bench, the sharp corner pressing into his palm. Mia couldn't be compared to women like his mother and Brooke. She stood apart by a million miles.

She didn't have a selfish bone in her body. She put others ahead of herself all the time. She'd nursed her mother, she'd risked her life to save the little girl from the crocodile and had rushed to defend a woman in danger. She'd even taken on Joe despite it being another job on a never-ending list.

He shook his head. If Mia had a fault it was that she cared too much. Care drove her every action, which was why she did crazy things like risking her life.

Why had she gone? Why had she left him? He stood up and leaned over the water fountain, splashing his face with water, using the coolness to try and clear his head.

Mia's mud-streaked face wafted through his mind. *I don't expect you to marry me, I don't expect or want anything from you.*

At the time lust had made him interpret those words as a gift. A woman who didn't want commitment but had wanted him had seemed too good to be true. He'd taken the gift with open arms. But why didn't a beautiful woman want the love of a man? She'd told him that her broken relationship had been for the best and she hadn't seemed distraught over it.

Think. He racked his brain, trying to remember conversations and her exact words. She'd been so stressed and uptight when she'd arrived on Kirra but that was reasonable considering she'd just come out of a year of death, losing her mother and brother within months of each other. She was certainly no stranger to grief, having coped with her father dying when she was younger.

I'm going to die. I know I'm going to die.

Her frantic words from two days ago tore at him. He'd heard her and dismissed the words as the frenzied ramblings of someone having a panic attack. Did she really believe she was going to die? He tried to shrug away the irrational thought but it kept hammering at him. Was that why she risked her life without thought for her own safety?

He started pacing again, needing the movement to think. Why did she think she was going to die? None of it made any sense. She was a healthy young woman with so much to offer. Sure, she had her own crazy little quirks, like writing down every little thing, but everyone has idiosyncrasies.

Her voice spoke softly in his head. *My mother died of dementia.*

He'd assumed her mother had been elderly but given that Mia was only twenty-six there was every possibility she'd been under the age of fifty.

Steven didn't want to marry into my family.

My brother's death is listed as a car accident.

The words started to pound in his head as the memory

of her eyes, totally blank and devoid of emotion after the crocodile attack, sucked the wind from his lungs.

With devastating clarity all the ducks lined up. Mia thought she had memory loss and the start of dementia. Her brother had taken his own life from fear of it. It had to be the explanation.

There are women out there who can make you happy. You need to get out there and meet them.

His heart thumped hard against his ribs and a glimmer of hope slowly unfolded deep inside him. Mia hadn't left him to hurt him. She'd left him to protect him.

Well, he wouldn't let her.

Decision spurred him on. He ran out of the park and back to the main road, looking for a taxi. Empty blacktop greeted him. He pulled out his phone and dialled a cab. He had to find her.

His brain had jerked from chaos to order as he ran through a plan. Just about every flight out of Darwin left after midnight and he had a really strong feeling she'd be heading south tonight. But she wasn't going anywhere if he had anything to do with it. He had twelve hours to find her. And if he failed in that time he'd lie in front of the plane if need be.

A cab came around the corner and pulled up beside him.

The driver leaned over and opened the door. 'Where to, mate?'

'The airport hotel.'

CHAPTER ELEVEN

Mɪᴀ lay on the bed, waiting for the air-conditioner to have an impact on the steaming air and cool the sauna that was her room. Now that the first part of her journey had been completed, her legs had turned to jelly.

The hotel staff had been very solicitous and made sure the phone, TV remote and water were within reach. They'd promised to bring her an early lunch so she could get a good rest this afternoon before her flight. Not that she had much of an appetite.

The clock showed twelve-thirty on the liquid display. Two hours since she'd left the hospital. Ninety minutes since Flynn would have arrived to collect her. She bit her lip and blinked rapidly, hating what she'd done but knowing she'd had scant choice.

If she'd waited and told him her plan, he wouldn't have let her leave. He didn't deserve the pain and hurt she'd just inflicted on him by disappearing, but more importantly he didn't deserve to lose a chunk of his life caring for her in a vegetative state.

Short-term pain for long-term gain, wasn't that what 'they' said? She prayed he would be OK. That he would find the love of a good woman, that…. Tears spilled down her cheeks. Why did life have to be this hard? She reached for a tissue and blew her nose.

She would *not* feel sorry for herself. She had a plan and working on that would keep her busy. She'd fly to Perth, find a menial job where she wasn't a danger to anyone and then investigate nursing homes. She'd find the best one for when she could no longer care for herself.

A knock sounded on her door. Lunch. She wearily swung her legs off the bed, holding her slinged arm close to her chest to avoid any jerking. 'Coming.'

She slid the chain back across its chase, turned the handle and opened the door. Silver spots shimmered in front of her eyes and she gripped the architrave for support.

'Hello, Mia.'

Flynn stood in the corridor, his face drawn, his clothing crumpled and his black hair spiked from being trammelled by fingers. His eyes flashed with a combination of fear and relief but when he spoke his voice only contained steely determination. 'I've come to talk to you. Don't even think of suggesting that I don't need to.'

His dishevelled look told her of the hell she'd put him through and her heart spasmed as her knees sagged beneath her. 'You weren't supposed to find me.'

'Well, I did.' His strong arms reached around her waist, supporting her. 'Come on, you need to be lying down.' The gruff words belied his tender touch as he guided her back to the bed.

Mia wanted to lean into him, wanted him to cradle her against his chest, but that would just make things worse. Make things harder than they already were.

The moment her bottom hit the mattress, Flynn stepped back and sat down in a chair a good metre away from her. 'Do you want to tell me why you're here?'

She drew in a long, deep breath. 'I'm on a late flight.'

'I gathered that. Can you tell me why?'

She closed her eyes for a moment, avoiding his penetrating gaze which threatened to undo her resolve. 'Remember when I told you I live day to day? Well, today I decided that while Kirra has been fun, it's time to go south.'

He crossed his arms across his broad chest and his cheeks sucked in as tension shot across his face. 'I don't believe you.'

Her heart started to hammer hard against her ribs. 'That's your prerogative.'

He leaned forward, his expression incisive. 'The Mia I've come to love wouldn't abandon her patients or Kirra on a whim.'

Her chest tightened. She'd been right. He really did love her. But she wouldn't let him. She needed to make him want to walk away from her. The fire of pain burned in her chest, vaporising her breath, and she gasped for air. 'Perhaps you don't know me as well as you think you do.'

His expression softened, love and affection radiating from him. 'I know you better than any woman I have ever loved. I know you better than you know yourself.'

'You don't.' The words rushed out in a feeble defence.

'I do.' His hands fell to his knees palms facing up. 'And I know you love me.'

The truth pummelled her like breakers over a reef but

she had to make him leave. 'You've got tickets on yourself. We were having a no-strings-attached affair, which you agreed to. Now it's over.'

'Look me in the eye and tell me you don't love me.'

His deep voice vibrated around her and she tried not to lose herself in warm hazel eyes. She dredged up the words to form the biggest lie of her life, but the denial wouldn't come. 'I'm going somewhere a lot cooler.'

'To die alone?'

Her heart stalled. He knew. How did he know? Panic surged in ever-increasing waves as words failed her completely.

'I know, Mia. Or at least I think I've worked it out. You believe you have an inherited disease like Huntington's.'

His words fell on her like an ice storm, jagged and sharp, giving her nowhere to hide. She swallowed and then looked straight at his empathetic face, and could no longer deny him the truth. 'Frontotemporal dementia.'

'Pick's disease.' He kept his gaze hooked with hers. 'How do you know you have it?'

'Because it killed my mother and my grandfather.' The words jetted out like water from a fire hose, released by his question. 'She started getting sick at forty. At first we thought she was bipolar with her impulsive shopping trips. But then she started doing things that are not associated with that disorder. She'd swear in social situations, using language I didn't even know she knew. She had always been Miss Manners but she began telling people exactly what she thought, no matter how hurtful. But the night she danced topless at the church Christmas party we knew something terrible was happening.'

'Did she have an MRI?' Flynn spoke quietly, his voice gently prompting.

She nodded slowly, remembering the day of the scan. 'Yes, and it showed atrophy of the brain that was consistent with her other symptoms.' Her breath shuddered out of her lungs. 'At that point a diagnosis of bipolar would have been a blessing.'

She hadn't told anyone about her mother but now she needed to. She needed Flynn to understand the true horror of the disease. 'Mum would listen to the same music over and over, hoard every newspaper that came into the house and have food jags. For weeks she would only eat carrots. She'd always been fastidious about her clothes and make-up but slowly she lost interest in herself and her personal hygiene slipped. That was when Michael and I decided she needed full-time care.'

'And you gave up your job to care for her?'

The anguish on his face reinforced her decision to head south. No one deserved to watch someone they love die a living death as they gradually lost everything that made them who they were. She plucked at the sheet beneath her, her fingers making little triangular shapes.

'Michael and I shared the care for a while but he...' She took a steadying breath. 'He couldn't handle it and left for Melbourne.' She dashed an errant tear off her face. 'Now do you understand? I've lived through this disease, every step of the way, with my mother and I won't let it destroy your life as well as mine.'

His eyes sparked with strength of purpose. 'It won't destroy my life. It would be an honour and privilege to care for you.' He ran his hand through his hair. 'Hasn't your time on Kirra taught you that a community cares for each other no matter what? Hell, the Kirri people are no strangers to hardship and if you do get sick then together we'll take care of you.'

'*If* I get sick?' His statement stunned her. 'Two days ago I threw myself into the path of a crocodile. I think that counts as impulsive and the early signs of the disease, don't you?'

He shook his head. 'Wanting to rescue people is part of who you are. It's why you're a nurse, why you cared for your mother, why you tried to get me to consider meeting other women.'

She shook her head furiously. 'No. No, it's not. You once said to me that impulse is action without thought and that the brain processes instinct differently. Well, it's obvious my brain can no longer tell the difference.'

He leaned forward. 'If you believe you're going to die sooner than later then it's normal human behaviour to take more risks.'

'If I believe I am going to die?' Her voice rose. 'This isn't a fairy-tale, Flynn. I have an autosomal dominant inherited disease. My mother isn't the only member of the family to die. Her father died of dementia and after her death Michael and I discovered she'd had a child three years before Michael was born and he died at four. My parents had *never* mentioned him.'

A frown wrinkled his high forehead. 'And you know for sure he died of FTD?'

She threw her hands up. 'Why would they never tell us about his existence if he'd died of something else? They must have been protecting us from the horrors ahead.'

'How old was your grandfather when he developed the disease?' He moved from his chair and sat down on the bed beside her, the mattress tilting her towards him.

She held herself stiffly, trying not to fall against him. 'I'm not certain. He and mum weren't that close but he died at seventy.'

He hesitated, as if he was forming a question in his mind. 'Did you and Michael have genetic testing once your mother was diagnosed?'

Her mother's doctor's voice boomed in her head, bringing back difficult memories. 'We were told that gene testing isn't recommended for us because they didn't consider we had a clear enough family history through generations.'

Flynn nodded his understanding. 'Even with family history, only six per cent of people have the predictive test because there are so many ethical concerns that it makes your head spin.'

She moistened her lips, remembering all too well that very scenario. 'Michael couldn't cope with any of it. He decided he was going to have the test but he suicided the night before he was to meet the genetic counsellor.'

Flynn slid his palm underneath her hand, letting it rest passively against hers, and yet it held her hand in place with such an amazing pull of energy that she couldn't lift her hand.

His voice spun around her as gentle as the touch of fleece. 'Even though your grandfather died of dementia too, it may have been a completely different type, especially as he was older. FTD isn't always inherited and your mother may have had a sporadic form. In that case, the predictive test wasn't going to be helpful for you.'

Her throat moved convulsively. 'But the time for me to have the test has passed anyway. I don't need a predictive test. I have the impulsive symptoms of the actual disease.' She gave a derisive cry. 'Did you know the only book I have read since mum died is *Emma*?'

'Because you love Jane Austen and reading it is a panacea. It calms you and makes you feel good.' His free hand came up to cradle her cheek. 'You've had a hellish time and I think you've interpreted the normal signs of stress and grief—the note taking, rereading books—as symptoms. I don't think you have early signs of FTD.'

She wanted to believe him and throw herself into his love and care, but that would only spin his world into a nightmare. She turned her head away from his touch and brought her free hand up to fiddle with the edge of her collar. 'And I think that you want too much to believe that I'm not sick so we can have a future together.'

For the first time his voice held a plea. 'Don't you want that?'

She turned her head back to see a tiny crack in his controlled demeanour, and pain shredded her heart. 'Of course I want that. I'd give anything to grow old with you and be surrounded by our grandchildren, but hope isn't enough to get us over the line.'

'"A woman who loves you stays with you."' Desperation clung to the words.

He was quoting her, using her own words against her. 'That's dirty pool, Flynn. I love you. I love you more than I have ever loved anyone, but I can't give you the children or the life that you deserve.' Her voice cracked as she made herself speak the words she most feared. 'Which is why I'm getting on that plane and leaving you.'

Flynn felt the last vestiges of his composure start to unravel. He'd resisted the overwhelming urge to haul her into his arms and never let her go. He'd tried to be the rational one, tried to get her to see that belief wasn't enough to make an irrefutable verdict.

He refused to lose her by letting her run away, but she was convinced she had FTD. He acknowledged there was a possibility but he was a scientist and he didn't deal in speculation. The only way to find out was to get a real diagnosis. 'I want you to have an MRI today.'

Her jaw tightened and she vehemently shook her head. 'There's no point having it today. I'll organise it when I'm settled down south.'

Desperation forced him to bargain. 'If you love me then you'll come back to Royal Darwin with me right now and have it today.'

A flash of dread flared in her eyes as a tremor shook her body. 'Only if you promise me that when they find frontal and temporal changes in my brain you'll respect my wishes. Let me get on that plane and not follow me.' She gripped his arm. 'Promise me you'll stop hiding and go out into the world and find the happiness you deserve.'

Every part of him rebelled at agreeing to her wishes. He wanted to keep her close to him, no matter the outcome. Life with Mia, even if they only had a few years together, was infinitely better than life without her.

But that wasn't the choice she was offering.

He had no real choice.

He didn't know the odds but for once he took a gamble and prayed the dice would fall in his favour.

Flynn had spent an hour on the phone and pulled in every favour he'd ever been owed. He'd managed to get both the consultant neurologist and radiologist as well as the radiographer all in the same place at the same time. And as much of a miracle as that was, even more so was that Mia hadn't fled.

She'd sat pale and silent, with white earpieces in place, listening to music. She hadn't spoken a word from the moment he'd triumphantly told her the scan would be at three p.m.

Now he paced back and forth in the small control room, watching through the glass as Mia, clutching the back of a standard hospital gown, was assisted up onto the 'bed' of the magnetic resonance imaging machine.

Callum Kelly, the radiographer, spoke gently in his soft Irish brogue. 'We're ready to start.'

'You'll need to wait outside, Flynn.' Doug Sanderson, the neurologist, clapped his brawny hand onto Flynn's shoulder, his smile tinged with the understanding of how difficult Flynn would find that request.

Right up to that moment Flynn had been confident that the MRI would bear out his strong feeling that Mia didn't have FTD. But as the bed started to move Mia slowly into the chamber of the machine, gut-wrenching dread poured through him, chilling him to his marrow. The unknown was ten times worse than the known.

She's here with you now but you'll lose her if she has the disease.

Perhaps the known was worse.

He walked toward the door and then spun back, grabbing the microphone that connected the control room to the machine, enabling the radiographer to communicate with the patient. Not caring a damn who else was in the room with him, he gripped it hard and flicked it on, raising it to his lips. 'Mia, I'm just outside, sweetheart. Remember, no matter what, I love you and I always will.'

Mia heard Flynn's voice and swallowed a sob. This amazing man had come into her life at the wrong time for both of them. Not that there would ever have been a right time for her. Although perhaps if she'd met him a few years ago, when she'd been unaware of the impact FTD had on her family, they would have had more time.

But then she would have died, leaving children and the huge possibility of having passed on the faulty gene. She never wanted anyone to experience the ravages of the disease or suffer the impact of watching a loved one fade away.

Flynn was in denial, which was why she'd agreed to the scan. She'd didn't need a scan to know the truth. She'd faced up to her future and accepted it. Now he needed to accept it as well, and the scan would be the proof he required.

'Mia?' The radiographer's voice came out of the speaker behind her head. 'How are you doing? How's your arm?'

'OK, thanks, Callum.' She blew out long slow breaths and kept her eyes closed, not wanting to open them and feel the claustrophobic presence of the machine that surrounded her. She'd had an individual meeting with the two doctors and the radiologist before the procedure. Doug Sanderson had asked a lot of questions about her family and her symptoms and she'd been exhausted at the end of it. Callum had been very sweet, checking with her twice that she didn't have a pacemaker or an aneurysm clip that would be damaged by exposure to the magnetic field.

'We've got your favourite CD to put on and the nurse has given you the buzzer. Press it if you need us to stop at any time.'

She nodded, enjoying the soothing lilt of Callum's voice but then realising he couldn't see her and she had to reply. 'Yes, I'm holding it in my good hand.'

'Right, then, we'll get started.'

The machine clicked as it changed positions every few minutes. Callum's voice would tell her when to hold still and when she could move. Her arm throbbed, her head pounded and the examination seemed to go on for ever.

Why is it taking so long?

Surely the atrophy would be evident from the first scan. Was there so much degeneration that they needed to map more than she'd expected? She chewed her lip and tried to still her mind by concentrating on the music, but it didn't work. Her mouth dried as her heart thumped hard, rushing adrenaline and agitation through her and making her feel all fluttery. Her fingers reached for the buzzer.

'We're nearly finished, Mia. Can you hang on just five minutes more?' Callum's voice sounded concerned.

Five minutes. She tried to moisten her mouth with her tongue. 'I don't know.'

'Mia, honey, remember when we climbed up that steep sand dune and sat on the top, watching the sun rise?' Flynn's voice unexpectedly came through the speaker. 'Picture that in your mind. We sat huddled together, the chill of the pre-dawn air unexpectedly cold, and then the sky changed from black to pink streaked with blue. As the light started to spread we saw a pod of dolphins diving in and out of the water, teasing us. We were stuck on land, while they had the freedom to explore the ocean far and wide.'

His velvet-smooth voice brought the image back clear and true. It was as if she was back on top of that dune with him. She could feel his arm around her, comforting and warm, as she cuddled into his shoulder. Her breathing slowed, her panic receded and she was able to follow Callum's final instructions.

Three minutes later it was all over. 'Well done to you, Mia. I'm sure that was a very long forty minutes. We're moving you out now and the nurse will take you back to the change room.' Callum paused for a moment. 'Mr Sanderson will meet you in the interview room.'

The bed started to move and a moment later Mia was able to sit up. She turned to look into the control room, hoping to catch a glimpse of Flynn, but it was one-way glass and she could only see the reflection of herself. Disappointment pulled at her. She needed as many glimpses of him as she could get because in a few hours she would never see him again.

'This way, Mia.' The nurse guided her back to the

change room and assisted her in putting on her dress and refitting the sling.

A few minutes later the nurse escorted her to the interview room, walking briskly at a typical nurse pace.

Mia wanted to walk slowly. Why walk quickly to bad news that she already knew and didn't need to be told? Why walk quickly to Flynn when she would just have to turn around and walk away from him?

Mia stepped inside the small room and started with surprise. It was empty. Where was Flynn? She'd expected him to meet her there.

Doug Sanderson arrived a moment later with a large yellow X-ray envelope tucked under his arm and holding two cups of coffee. He passed one to her. 'Flynn said you liked it strong.'

'Thanks.' She peeled the top back and breathed in the aroma. How much longer did she have before she wouldn't be able to associate that amazing bouquet with coffee? She pushed the thought away. 'Where's Flynn?'

'He's outside.' Doug sat down on the opposite couch, the yellow envelope sliding to the floor.

'On the phone?' She couldn't imagine any other reason that would prevent him from being with her.

Doug shook his head. 'No, he's waiting. Technically, he isn't next of kin and he didn't presume that you would want him to be in here with you.'

Hurt and bewilderment merged. 'But that's crazy.'

'Is it?' The doctor raised his craggy brows. 'You told him that if you had FTD you didn't want him in your life.' Doug sipped his coffee as if he was letting his words sink in.

The last unrealistic strand of hope inside her snapped. 'So it's true. I do have FTD and he knows it.' Her voice stumbled as tears pricked the back of her eyes.

'I haven't given you a diagnosis yet, Mia, and Flynn hasn't see the results. We sent Flynn out of the control room and only called him back when you started to get agitated.' Peter's expression was that of a stern father. 'I'm asking you, do you want Flynn here with you now when you're prepared to cut him out of your life if the news is bad?'

Frustration surged. Why didn't anyone understand her motives? 'But that's for his own good.'

Peter shrugged. 'So your brand of love only works in the good times?'

Mia blinked. She'd never met a neurologist who doubled as a relationship counsellor. 'No!' Her indignation bounced off the walls. 'But—'

He cut her off. 'For some couples, love only works in the good times, but Flynn is made of sterner stuff than that. Did it ever occur to you that your action of leaving, which you think is altruistic, is actually selfish? You're denying a man who loves you the chance to live his life the way he chooses to.'

A woman who loves you won't walk away.

She'd dished out pat advice to Flynn and she hadn't been able to take it herself. She didn't want to leave him but she had to protect him. Protect him from what she'd slowly become. How was that selfish?

She laced her fingers tightly in her lap as her thoughts swirled. Did she have the right to tell Flynn he couldn't care for her? How would she have felt if her mother had told her the same thing?

She would have hated it. She would have railed against it and refused to accept it. Understanding stormed in. She didn't have the right to tell Flynn how to handle her illness or put parameters on his love. She loved him and she needed to allow him to love her his way.

She struggled to her feet and pulled open the door.

The moment she stepped into the corridor she saw Flynn push himself off the wall he'd been leaning against. Strain showed clearly on his face, in his hollow cheeks and the deep lines bracketing his mouth.

Her heart expanded in love as she worked to accept that the pain this situation was causing him was less than the pain she would inflict on his heart if she left.

She reached her good arm out toward him. 'Flynn, before I find out the results I… There's something I have to say.'

Flynn took three steps and pulled her gently into his arms, being careful not to knock her injured arm. He buried his face in her hair, breathing in her scent, knowing that it might be the last time he was able to do it. Waiting had been pure agony. It still was but at least he could hold her.

He may have been able to pull strings to get the MRI but the team had fittingly respected Mia's right to hear the diagnosis before anyone else.

She gazed up at him, determination clear in her eyes. 'I love you, Flynn Harrington, and I know you love me.' She sucked in a quick breath. 'But are you absolutely certain you really want to care for me if I do have FTD?'

A kernel of optimism tried to shoot but he dared not hope that she'd changed her mind. 'Will you let me?'

She bit her lip and nodded. 'I'm so sorry that I've put you through this hell.' A tear rolled down her cheek. 'I thought by leaving I was doing the right thing, but if it was the other way around I would hate it if you insisted I leave you.'

Joy surged through him and he traced his finger down her cheek. 'I love you, Mia. Whatever we face, we'll face it together. Are you ready?'

She shuddered against him and then tossed her head up, strands of her hair caressing his face. She caught his hand, gripping it hard. 'It's time. Let's do this.'

Doug sat them down. 'As a couple there are some things you need to know about this disease. Forty per cent of FTD is believed to have a genetic component, which leaves sixty percent with no apparent hereditary link.'

Mia concentrated hard on Doug's sonorous voice, trying to listen when most of her was screaming, *Just tell me the results.*

Flynn's hand gave her a reassuring squeeze, which told her he felt exactly the same.

'Your family history doesn't give a clear genetic link but it is totally understandable, after the trauma you have been through and the vagaries of your grandfather and older brother's deaths, for you to believe a link is probable.' He stood up and turned on the light box, inserting the grey scans under the clip. He then beckoned them both over.

'As you can see here and here and here…' he tapped the scans with his pen '…there are absolutely no signs of atrophy in your brain. It's as healthy as you would expect for someone of your age.'

His words broke over her and every part of her went numb. White noise roared in her head. She couldn't think, she couldn't feel.

She'd been so certain.

She'd been so *wrong*.

Flynn's arm slid around her, his voice soft in her ear. 'Mia, darling, you're well.'

She held his arm hard against her waist, needing his touch and support as her final fear erupted. 'What about my future and children?'

Doug responded instantly, as if he'd anticipated the question. 'Given the circumstances and the fact that you lack a real history but your mother definitely had FTD, I think that the gene test will give you peace of mind. It will most likely prove to you that your mother was in the sixty per cent basket and had sporadic FTD.'

Her eyes scanned Flynn's face, knowing how much he wanted children. 'If I do have the gene, I don't want to risk passing it on to a child.'

He smiled at her, his face full of love and understanding. 'Then we'll adopt. We'll foster kids; we'll help out some of the kids on Kirra. Whatever happens, we'll work it out together. We're going to have a fabulous life together.'

Her heart almost burst with love for this incredible man who adored and loved her despite the unknown.

Peter scrawled words on a referral pad. 'Flynn, take this lovely young women on a holiday to Brisbane; take in the sights, some genetic counselling and a gene test.

Then come back and start the rest of your lives.' He shook both their hands and left the room.

Flynn cradled her close. 'When do you want to leave for Brisbane?'

She snuggled in, feeling his heart beating under her hand, still not quite believing that she had a wonderful future ahead of her with this man. 'Can you hire a plane and fly us down now?'

He grinned and kissed her hard and fast. 'Works for me.'

EPILOGUE

THE outback sun shone white against an expansive blue sky. The sea lapped gently on the shore and across the dirt road the cream weatherboard church with its wooden louvres groaned against its stilts as the capacity crowd filled the pews. This was a wedding everyone had waited months for. Now the dry season and the day for a true celebration had arrived.

The sanctuary walls were decorated with the fine lines of Kirri cross-hatching and dots, their distinctive earthy red yellow and white warming the church. Motifs of pelicans, fish, turtles, crocodiles and crabs linked the Kirri with their land and fused two cultures.

The groom stood at ease at the altar, smiling widely at everyone, with no trace of the usual pre-wedding nerves.

'Flynn, is my tie done right?' Walter asked anxiously as he plunged his hand down into his suit pocket for the third time in as many minutes.

Flynn laughed at the role reversal—usually the best man was reassuring the groom. 'Mate, your tie is fine and that ring is still in your pocket just like it was a moment ago.' He squeezed Walter's shoulder. 'Relax and enjoy. After what Mia and I have been through, today is just one big celebration. If there are a few fluffed lines and dropped rings, it doesn't matter.'

The chants of Kirri men floated through the windows, their clapping sticks beating rhythmically. Inside the church the organ lay silent. Instead, at the sound of the sticks the glorious strains of trumpet and strings soared to a crescendo. The bride had arrived.

Flynn turned, his eyes glued to the door, not wanting to miss a moment of Mia walking toward him as his bride.

She stepped into the doorway and paused. Susie and Jenny fussed behind her, their hands gentle and caring against the long, white silk jacket, delicately hand-painted with silver Kirri designs.

Holding a fragrant bouquet of frangipani, Mia raised her head, hooked her gaze to Flynn's and smiled. Her gaze never wavered as she glided down the aisle toward him.

Her full-length straight dress was stunning in its simplicity, accentuating every delightful curve, including the hint of tiny bump that only he and Mia knew about—the ultimate wedding gift for them both. It took every ounce of Flynn's self-control not to stride up the aisle and meet her. But finally her hand touched his arm.

He covered her hand with his. 'You look amazing.'

'Thank you.' Her eyes sparkled with a teasing look. 'I'm warning you, though, this jacket makes this the re-spectable church version of the dress.'

He glanced down, catching a hint of golden thigh as the jacket swung sideways. 'I can't wait for the recep-tion, then.'

She laughed, her eyes full of joy and free of shadows.

He brushed the side of her cheek with his forefinger, wondering at the gift that had come his way when Mia had sought refuge on the island. 'In fact, I can't wait to start the rest of our lives. We have so many wonderful adventures ahead of us.'

Then he broke protocol and in front of the minister, his best man and a full church he swung Mia into his arms and kissed her, making her his wife.

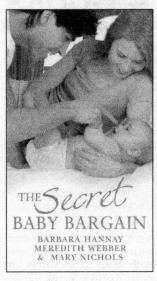

FREE!

4 Books
and a surprise gift!

We would like to take this opportunity to thank you for reading this Mills & Boon® book by offering you the chance to take FOUR more specially selected titles from the Medical™ series absolutely FREE! We're also making this offer to introduce you to the benefits of the Mills & Boon® Book Club™—

- ★ **FREE home delivery**
- ★ **FREE gifts and competitions**
- ★ **FREE monthly Newsletter**
- ★ **Exclusive Mills & Boon Book Club offers**
- ★ **Books available before they're in the shops**

Accepting these FREE books and gift places you under no obligation to buy, you may cancel at any time, even after receiving your free shipment. Simply complete your details below and return the entire page to the address below. You don't even need a stamp!

YES! Please send me 4 free Medical books and a surprise gift. I understand that unless you hear from me, I will receive 6 superb new titles every month for just £2.99 each, postage and packing free. I am under no obligation to purchase any books and may cancel my subscription at any time. The free books and gift will be mine to keep in any case.

M9ZEF

Ms/Mrs/Miss/Mr ....Initials.................................
BLOCK CAPITALS PLEASE
Surname ....
Address...

....
....Postcode ....

Send this whole page to:
UK: FREEPOST CN81, Croydon, CR9 3WZ